THE CONFESSIONS OF JUDAS

THE CONFESSIONS OF JUDAS

Michael Dickinson

Copyright ©2000 by Michael Dickinson.

ISBN #:   Softcover   0-7388-2066-0

All rights reserved. No part of this book may be reproduced or transmitted in any form or by any means, electronic or mechanical, including photocopying, recording, or by any information storage and retrieval system, without permission in writing from the copyright owner.

This is a work of fiction. Names, characters, places and incidents either are the product of the author's imagination or are used fictitiously, and any resemblance to any actual persons, living or dead, events, or locales is entirely coincidental.

This book was printed in the United States of America.

To order additional copies of this book, contact:
Xlibris Corporation
1-888-7-XLIBRIS
www.Xlibris.com
Orders@Xlibris.com

The Son of man goeth as it is written of him: but woe unto that man by whom the Son of man is betrayed! It had been good for that man if he had not been born.
Matthew 26:24

The document you are about to read was passed on to me by an unnamed contact who works in the Vatican. He claims it to be the translation of a manuscript that has been kept there under conditions of strict secrecy for several centuries.

Apart from changing a few archaic words and phrases to make it more understandable to a modern reader, I have interfered with the script as little as possible.

It is not for me to say whether the document is authentic or not – I leave you to make your own decision. Read it with an open mind.

Michael Dickinson Istanbul 2000

> *Now this man purchased a field with the reward of his iniquity; and falling headlong, he burst asunder in the midst, and all his bowels gushed out.*
> Acts 1:18

> *And he cast down the pieces of silver in the temple, and departed, and went and hanged himself*
> Matthew 27.5

Jezebel. That's the name I've given the spider that hangs in the web above my head. She lolls there, indolent harlot, her legs spread, awaiting the clients attracted in from the dark outside by the inviting glow of my lamp. Moths, beetles, mosquitoes: she isn't fussy; she caters to all tastes. Or they cater to hers, to speak more truly, the bloated darling. A perfect hostess, she quickly calms the nerves of her fluttering guests with a stunning kiss and gently tucks them up tight in freshly spun silken thread until ready for her undivided attention at an intimate supper. Thanks to her caterer pimp, Jezebel's larder is always full, but what thanks do I get? None, of course. She isn't even aware of my existence. Nobody is, except Martha.

I crouch here, cross-legged in the cave, surrounded on all sides by rock. The shadows cast by the wavering flame of the lamp in the pits and grooves of the hewn walls mesmerize me. They sway and undulate, forming eyebrows, mouths, shrugs and shapes, people and places, parading my past before my eyes. Mistakes. Horrors . . . God bless Martha for allowing me the means to distract myself with this papyrus, stylus and ink. Without them, I believe the rock would soak me into it and I would become mad, trapped within memories. My shadow peeps over my shoulder, an impatient demon waiting for me to finish my scribbling and come away with him to Hell.

At night the silence is unbearable. During the day I can hear the grinding of the oil-press and the occasional laughter of the workers. I hate the sound of laughter! How can anyone laugh? What is there to laugh about? Nothing. I know that I will never laugh again.

It is so quiet at night that sometimes the sound of my breathing and the blood throbbing in my temples are the only reminders that I am not deaf. They, and the malignant whine of the mosquitoes settling on my face, and the slap of my hand thwarting their chance to sting. Occasionally, the distant howling of a dog, and echoing howls in answer, faint and far away. Dogs have a remarkable sense of hearing. If we could learn their language and teach them to understand us, there would be no more need for letters or messengers. You would just need to dictate the message to a cur, and it would be barked from one to another throughout the country in less than an hour.

The Romans would forbid it, of course. Who know what message of rebellion might be being broadcast? Besides that, if everybody used the dog-system at the same time, there would such be a jumbled continual blare of growls and howls that nothing would be decipherable. Perhaps it's better left alone.

I ramble on about spiders and dogs in a vain attempt to stop my thoughts. Why can I not still them? What bliss it would be to be thoughtless, like Jezebel couched up there! Just being, without memories, without the nagging conscience, continually chattering, accusing, and condemning! To be nothing. What I wouldn't give to be nothing!

The air is still and thick, like warm blood. My shirt sticks to my back with sweat; my hair and beard hang in wet coils. The sky outside is a black and stagnant sea; the stars are luminous jellyfish in its depths. My bones ache, my legs are numb, cramped as I am here, confined. What about a walk, a short stroll out there under the olive trees to stretch my limbs and inhale the odors of the earth? It is past midnight; no one is about. In fact, why do I not go now, leave and walk away, away and leave it all behind like he did? I cannot stay here forever in this tomb. Let me have some more of life before I am laid in a grave of my own! But no. Not yet. Let me wait just a little longer. Something is going to happen. It isn't the end yet. It can't be.

A casual walk could cost my life. Admittedly, the village is asleep at this hour, but out there in the dark, curled up at the foot of a tree, might lie a sleeping dog which would awake and signal in the language that human beings *do* understand. Not the undecipherable lonely howl, but the strident, snarling warning that arouses households. Stranger! Prowler! Burglar! Up they would spring from their beds and run with lamps and cudgels, to find me cornered, fending off the savage brute and trying to hide my face from the cruel, revealing light.

"You! Judas! Still alive! You are supposed to be dead! For what you have done you should be dead! If you won't do it yourself, we'll do it for you!"

And they advance on me with their heavy sticks, showering me with stones and spittle, screaming curses and accusations.

"Spy! Traitor! Murderer!"

No. I won't risk my life for a mere stroll. When I walk, I'll walk for good. Until then I am safe here in the tomb.

I live like a beast in its lair. The stone is pushed aside just wide enough for a man to squeeze through, but Martha, being small, enters easily when she brings my food and wine at night, and a clean pot to replace the one I have soiled during the day. How ashamed I am to submit her to such a degrading task, but she says it is nothing compared to the filth I performed in Jerusalem. She comes and goes in brisk silence, but she cannot conceal her bitterness and disgust for me. Like everybody else, she believes that I am a filthy damned traitor, and she must continue to believe it. I cannot tell her the truth. To protect the Master's reputation, I must remain mute and accept the role of villain.

But she alone knows that I am still alive. The others believe that I killed myself for what I did, hanged myself on a tree in a deserted grove, and am rotting there, unmourned and unburied. Sometimes I think that is what I should have done, instead of running and groveling here, pleading with her to conceal me. She hates me now, but I knew she would take me in, that she would force herself to do as she would be done by.

The tomb was Martha's idea. Cut into the cliff, far down at the end of the garden, out of sight of the house and olive-press, sheltered by the grove and conveniently empty after the resurrection of Lazarus. That miraculous night! Last week, Martha brought some curious visitors down, and they stood outside marveling while she related the story, me inside, rigid, hardly daring to breathe. How Lazarus had fallen ill and died, been anointed and entombed, and three days later the Master had arrived, ordered the covering stone to be removed, and called Lazarus to return to life. Out he had come, restored, alive, returned from death! Yes indeed, there had been many witnesses. A miracle had taken place.

Martha knew that I was listening to her commentary from inside, and aware of the irony in her tone, but I was nevertheless proud of her. She is a true disciple and would never betray the secret behind her brother's raising. Sometimes I feel I could almost trust her with the rest. She would love me again. But it is impossible. Nobody must know. Ever . . .

Martha lives alone now. News of his miracle brought curiosity seekers down from Jerusalem to wonder at Lazarus. One, a rich widow, offered herself in marriage, and he accepted. He moved to her mansion in the city and manages her inherited spice business. Mary has run off again. Martha says she went insane after the crucifixion, claiming that she had seen the Master and spoken to him. She left home to find and follow him. Would that I could do the same! I would gladly die for just one last glimpse. Even from a distance, just to know that he is alive and well.

How long have I been here? It can't be more than a fortnight, but it feels like an eternity. Days and nights stretch out like an endless chain. I doze during the days, but nightmares of the Master's frowning face and bitter words of rejection always come and I awake crying his name. I pray to God then, for I know that He understands and forgives me, but that is not enough. It is the Master's love and forgiveness I crave. I am in Hell without it.

But sometimes my well of sorrow bubbles up with anger and indignation at the way I have been treated. Without me everything would have come to naught. He owes me his very life! But what was my reward? No thanks. Anger. Hateful abuse. And banishment from his sight forever. If he had followed my advice and shown himself when I suggested, how swiftly the word would have spread! He would be King even now, accepted as the Messiah by hundreds and thousands. What do we have instead? The flock without the shepherd, the leader disappeared to God knows where, the mission unfulfilled. What was the point of it all? It could have culminated in the ultimate glory if he had listened to me. Useless. Pointless.

Now I must try to sleep and quell these sinful and rebellious thoughts. I am still devoted to you, Master. But I know that what I did was right. I refuse to accept your condemnation. If I had the chance to live through it all again there is nothing I would change, though sometimes, perhaps, I cannot help but wish . . . if only . . .

Martha has just brought me the most incredible news! Her voice shook with incredulity as she told me that Peter had called this afternoon on the way to Jerusalem. He and the brothers are back—preaching the resurrection! After the arrest in the Garden of Gethsemane they had fled the city and returned to Galilee, fearing for their lives, but a few days later the Master appeared and spoke to them while they were fishing. He showed them the wounds in his hands and told Peter to return with the others to Jerusalem, preach the gospel, spread the news of his resurrection, baptize and win new converts. He said he was going away for a time, but expected to find a rich harvest from their labors on his return. Then he departed, warning them not to follow or try to find him.

Yes! He has done it! The mission has begun again! And although I can no longer take part in it myself, the news has made a new man of me.

Mary had also appeared in Galilee shortly after, saying that she was following the Master, and no one could stop her. To keep him in sight would be enough for her, and she hoped that a day might come when he would need and accept her. Then, bidding farewell, she had set off in the same direction.

Peter says the brothers' new zeal is boundless. They preach tirelessly and are not afraid. Their witness of the risen Master has given them unquenchable courage.

Peter preaches with them. Leads them. Proclaims the resurrection. And yet he knows the truth. Not everything, of course, but enough. Oh what great faith! What devotion! To spread the lie for love of the Master! May God bless him and protect him in his endeavors!

Peter is the only one who knows that I am not a traitor. He knows, but his understanding is not complete. He was puzzled by the events of that night. Could I not share the secret with him and die uncursed by at least one good man? He would not lose faith, but agree that I had done the only thing to save the Master.

Yes. Peter must know my story. I shall write it down. I have the means here, the papyrus and the ink. He, only he, will read it. Then the manuscript must be destroyed. I am certain that he would never reveal the secret, even under torture.

And so, salutations to you my beloved brother Peter! After you have read this, things that have puzzled you will become clear. You will know that, far from being the treacherous villain I have been painted, I am in fact a hero, a saint, worthy of the highest praise and respect!

I beseech you that if and when the Master returns, you will beg forgiveness for all the hurt that I caused him. Please kiss him for me. Give him the belated kiss he expected from me that I gave to another . . .

Every Kingdom divided against itself is brought to desolation; and every city or house divided against itself shall nor stand . . .
Matthew 12:25

First I should tell you a little about myself. We lived and worked together, but we did not really know much about each other's lives, or the causes that brought us to devote our lives to the Master. Our identities did not matter. It was his message that we carried which was of the greatest importance.

My mother died giving birth to me in the village of Kerioth, in Judea—hence my name Iscariot. I don't remember my father, who was a potter, but I'm told he blamed me for my mother's death and couldn't stand the sight of me, so I was sent to be brought up in Bethany in the household of his brother, my Uncle Bartholomew, where I was treated as one of the family. He was a fairly well off wine merchant, and I lacked for nothing.

As a boy, I was so proud of my name. Judas! My grandfather chose it for me. He was a great story-teller and I would hold my breath and listen enthralled whenever he related the tale of my namesake, Judas the Galilean, who had gathered an army of followers and risen up to drive the Roman occupiers out of our country. I never tired of hearing the story, and was amazed by the fact that my grandfather, though a babe in arms at the time, had been alive in those days. He swore that had he been a man, he would have joined with Judas in his attempt to liberate the land.

My best friend Lazarus and I became obsessed with the tale, and encouraged our playmates to join in our favourite game—"Zealots versus Romans", which we played every day in the dusty backstreets. My heart would swell with pride whenever I was chosen to play the role of my namesake, Judas, and my voice trembled with real passion as I rallied my followers.

"Our only duty is to God! We are free! Only through discontent, only through action, can the Messiah, the promised liberator, be found!"

And then we would fight tirelessly with our little wooden swords. Passing adults smiled or frowned at our antics, little realizing that their freedom the liberty of their country depended upon the outcome of our mock skirmishes.

But however hard we fought, the outcome was a foregone conclusion, for our game stuck ruthlessly to the tragic facts of history, and we were powerless to change it. The boy playing the part of the Roman commander, Varus, would always be the victor, and my little gang of four or five would be hung up on makeshift crosses to represent the two thousand rebels who had been truly crucified, while Judas escaped to the safety of Lebanon. Brief hope and elation flickered for a while as a fresh campaign was planned there, but the game would always end as it did in life, with the capture of Judas, his transportation in chains to Rome, and his own ignoble crucifixion there. The game over, we would part soberly and make our ways home, my thoughts a mixture of depression and hope. Judas the Galilean had failed, but his example was still treasured in many a heart. The Roman yoke must be thrown from our necks some day. Then, and only then, could the glorious reign of the Messiah begin.

I grew older, and like other boys, I grew out of such games. School took their place, the memorizing of the Torah, the putting on of manhood.

Time slips through our fingers like water. Schooling finished. Dear old grandfather went the way of all flesh. My Uncle Bartholomew made me a partner of his small but flourishing wine business. I was a responsible adult. But my rebellious ideals remained those of my childhood, although I had learned the danger of carelessly revealing them to others.

I was not content with mere silent grudging acceptance of the occupation, like my uncle and cousins, and I was sickened by the example of our religious leaders, who seemed to fawn on the Roman overlords like pet dogs. There had to be something we could do to gain our freedom. My heart would burn with impotent rage whenever a garrison of Roman soldiers raised the dust tramping through Bethany on the way to Jerusalem, or when I had to accompany my uncle to the tax collector to pay our debt to Caesar. Everywhere I could see the poverty and subjection of my people, while the conquerors lived off the fat of the land.

There were times on a summer night as I lay out on our flat roof under the stars when I would become intoxicated by wild, bitter dreams. I would become a Zealot! I would take up arms like Judas the Galilean before me and drive the Roman dogs yelping into the sea! What had I to lose but my life? But then I would shudder as I remembered the outcome of my grandfather's tale, and imagined myself groaning and wracked in the agony of the slow and terrible death of the cross. As common an execution now as it was then for rebels against Roman rule. I had seen them hanging there outside the walls of the city. It sometimes takes them days to die. My zeal was not strong enough to face that. Rather than suffering physically, I must bear it silently, a canker in my soul. In shame I had to admit that I was no hero. I was afraid of them. A coward.

My friendship with Lazarus continued. Being neighbors, we spent nearly every day together at my house or his, sitting in the courtyard during the day, or up on the roof in the evening, drinking wine and philosophizing. Armed uprising was no longer one of our topics. That was too dangerous a subject, even among friends. Instead we talked of the expected Messiah; when he would come and what he would be like; the corruption of the Sadducees and the sanctimoniousness of the Pharisees. We agreed on most points and rarely argued.

Lazarus was also from a fairly well off family. They had an olive grove and operated an oil-press in their garden. Business was good. His two sisters, Martha and Mary, although they never joined in our discussions, would often sit with us and listen as they sewed or prepared the evening meal. Martha was the older, a plain girl with a sweet and gentle disposition. Mary, on the other hand, was beautiful to behold, but of a fiery and sullen nature. I don't believe I ever saw her smile in those days.

My Uncle Bartholomew died, leaving me in charge of the wine business with my two younger cousins. We continued a steadily flourishing trade, even numbering Romans from the city among our regular clients. Although my heart was bitter, our wine was sweet.

I became engaged to Martha. The match was to be solemnized the following year. Although love had nothing to do with it, I was not averse to the idea of marriage. Tradition had to be conformed with. Like my uncle and father and grandfather before me, I must produce offspring, and when I was gone they would continue the process, passing on the wine business from generation to generation. Each in their turn to be crushed under the grinding heel of Rome.

Then one day news came to Bethany that quickened my heart. A traveler, passing through the village on his way to Jerusalem, sat with the idlers under the shade of the tamarisks and related what he had seen and heard in the region of Bethabara. A man of wild appearance had appeared there on the banks of the River Jordan announcing that the 'Kingdom of Heaven' was at hand, and calling for the people to repent. He took those who accepted his message down into the river and immersed them in the water, claiming to be washing their souls clean as well as their bodies if they were truly repentant of their sins. Rumor had it that he was the fabled Elijah, come again to deliver the people from the evil of foreign domination and announce the Day of Vengeance. Some even proclaimed that he was the Messiah. His name was John.

> *For I say unto you, Among those that are born of women there is nor a greater prophet than John the Baptist: but he that is least in the kingdom of God is greater than he.*
> Luke 7:28

Could he be the one? Had the Deliverer come at last? I was overcome with an ardent desire to see him, but was not about to broadcast my hopes to all and sundry. Apart from the fear of spies and informers who would cleverly try to trap the careless into betraying themselves in conversation, I didn't want to be made to look a fool if John turned out to be nothing more than just another manic preacher.

Using the excuse that I was going on a business trip to discuss a deal with a prospective client in a distant village, I set out for Bethabara with high expectations.

It appeared that I was not the only one who had heard the news, for I met others on the road making the pilgrimage to see and hear "the Baptiser", as they called him, families, groups, and loners like myself. I fell into company with one of the latter, a tough farmer who said he had come to see if what he had heard was true, that one of the expected prophets had at last come out into the open. He had heard that John was not one to mince his words. He savagely criticized the rich and declaimed against King Herod, calling his marriage adulterous and his wife a whore. I replied guardedly, claiming mere curiosity as the motive for my journey.

We met other pilgrims returning from Bethabara, both the satisfied and the disillusioned. My ears were open to the words of the hopeful. Some had been baptized by John and claimed that their sins had been washed away. They felt born anew and prepared for the coming kingdom. They said that he preached against property. All was to be shared. Poverty would be a thing of the past. They described John as angry and fierce, but totally sincere. He was inspired.

I could not, however, ignore the views of others that described him as a madman possessed by a demon. Some asked what good were words and water when it was deeds and action that was needed to stir up the people. And there were others who said that he was signing his own death warrant with the sedition he preached. It would not be long before the authorities realized the threat he was posing and stepped in to put a stop to him.

The sight that met us when we finally arrived at the river rather disgusted me. It was like a funfair. Sellers of sweets and souvenirs moved among the chattering crowds, hawking their wares. Groups of rich society folk, conspicuous in their ostentatious finery, held little parties, aloof from the common people around them. It was a great novelty for them to be condemned in public, and they giggled and nodded at John's diatribe, daring each other to go down the riverbank to repent and be baptized, but there was no sign of true contrition on their faces as they emerged from their ducking, simpering and waving to their applauding friends. Poor people, on the other hand, reacted with great sincerity, singing psalms and raising their arms in joy as they waded to the shore.

John himself was a sight to behold. Almost black from the sun, with matted locks and grizzled beard, half-naked in a goat skin loincloth, he stood up to his thighs in the muddy swirling water, crying out in a cracked, strident voice for sinners to repent and come to him to be shriven. His glaring eyes and knotted brow held no invitation for me, but I eased my way closer through the crowd, the better to hear him. After my long journey, surely there was something I might gain from his wild talk that would profit my soul.

As I drew nearer, I saw that he was in dispute with a group of Pharisee priests standing on the bank. John was ranting at them, his bony fingers pointing accusingly. He called them vipers, and declared that the axe had been laid to the root of the tree and all that did not yield good fruit would he hewn down and cast into the fire. The Pharisees bristled with outrage and demanded to know who he thought he was. His answer, after a short pause, relieved more than disappointed me. He said he was not the Messiah.

One demanded to know if he was supposed to be Elijah. John said he was not. Was he a prophet? He was not. Looking at his colleagues in triumph and preening himself on his apparently successful interrogation, the Pharisee turned to John with a slightly gentler air, as though talking to an idiot, and asked what it was then that he claimed to be, for they were to deliver a report on him to the temple authorities.

John's voice rose in a ringing bellow, replying that he was the voice of one crying in the wilderness for the way to be made straight for the Lord, as prophesied by Isaiah.

There was a brief silence before one of the other priests imperiously inquired what gave him the right to baptize, if he was neither the Christ nor Elijah, nor even a prophet? Reaching down, John took a palmful of water and studied it silently. Then looking up, he declared that one stronger than he was coming, whose very sandals he was not worthy to untie. And that man would baptize not with water, but with fire.

At that moment, as though conjured, a burning gust of wind blew down, raising the dust in stinging swirls along the riverside and causing many to cover their eyes in protection. At the same instant, a half-naked figure stepped into the water and waded out towards John. The sky grew yellow, as though a storm were coming. The Pharisees turned to go, pulling their headscarves over mouths and nostrils. One shouted threateningly across the water that they had heard enough from him, but that he would certainly be hearing more from them.

John appeared not to hear them, for he had drawn the man who had come to him further out into the middle of the river, where they stood waist-deep, the man's elbows firmly gripped in

John's hands. They stared fixedly into one another's eyes. John's lips were moving and the man's moved in reply, but they were too far away to be heard. I could not help but compare their appearances. John was emaciated, big-boned and prematurely wrinkled by the sun. The stranger, on the other hand, was pale, his body well formed and slender, a calm sureness and majesty about his bearing. The expression of his face, above all, even from afar, struck me with its serenity and sincerity, a sharp contrast with the demonic glare of the Baptist's.

Their conference ended, and they gazed so long and intently into each other's eyes that the crowd on the bank, who had been muttering oaths against the scorching wind and dust, gradually fell silent and focussed their attention on them, waiting for something to happen. Suddenly the Baptiser's hands flew up abruptly and plunged the man down by the shoulders, holding him forcefully under the brown turbulent water as though drowning him. In the same instant the wind ceased, the sky cleared to a pale blue, and the threatening storm was gone. As the man broke to the surface gasping for breath, a flock of doves released from a cage by a boy on the bankside whirred up and spiraled above the figures in the river before getting their bearings and flying off homeward. The scene we had witnessed seemed magical, and I could not help joining in the applause as the stranger staggered out of the water towards us. He glanced at me briefly with his dark brown eyes as he passed, and a feeling I had never experienced before made me catch my breath. I cannot explain it. It was in my belly – as though I had dropped from a great height. For a second I thought that I might faint. It was the Master.

It was the first time I had laid eyes on him. Yet somehow I knew right there and then that he only had to ask me and I would follow him anywhere and do anything he bade me do. He was the one that I had been searching for without knowing it. With him my life would be fulfilled. I knew then that I would not go down to be baptized by John. It was no longer necessary. I had found the one who would clean and heal us all.

Shaking off the elated daze that had fallen upon me, I struggled through the throng in the direction he had taken, wondering what I would say when I found him. But he was gone. After fruitlessly questioning many, I was told by a careworn woman with a child at her breast that she had seen the man I described putting on his garments and hurrying away, as thought urgently called elsewhere.

I returned to Bethany, my hopes in John unfulfilled. I kept my pilgrimage a secret, even from Lazarus, whom I went to visit as soon as I had washed off the sweat and dust of travel.

I found his house in turmoil. Mary had disappeared. The family had woken that morning to find her gone without a word. She had taken some clothes and a little money and left secretly in the night while they slept. Lazarus was grim-faced and Martha was sobbing. Their father, Simon, rocked backwards and forwards, hugging himself and moaning about the shame she had brought upon the family.

Speculating on where she might have gone and why, Lazarus aired his suspicions. The previous day a squadron of Roman soldiers had passed through the village, and he had seen Mary giving one of them wine at the house door, talking and laughing, her hair uncovered. Lazarus had admonished her sharply and slapped her face, at which Mary had flown into a rage, stamping her feet, complaining that women were no more than the chattels of men, condemned to a life of servitude and drudgery, and she had had enough of it. After Lazarus had slapped her again, she had stormed off to her chamber, not to be seen again. Martha's wails increased when Lazarus said he believed she might have followed the Roman soldiers and joined the traitorous band of whores who straggled after them, catering to their lust. Simon silenced him with a curse and announced that Mary's name was not to be mentioned in their house as long as he lived.

They say misfortunes do not come singly, and they certainly seemed to have come home to roost on Lazarus and his family. A few weeks later, symptoms of the dreaded leprosy were detected in Simon, and he was sent away to end his life in a colony, leaving his heavy-hearted son to take over the running of the olive.press.

News reached the village that John had been arrested, charged with treason for speaking out against Herod's adulterous marriage and for calling his wife a whore. The Pharisees had fulfilled their promise. And although I pitied John and resented his betrayal, I felt no great loss, having seen him and sensed that he was not the one who would fulfil out hopes of deliverance.

Instead, not a day went by when I did not think of the man that I had seen John baptize. I could recall perfectly the way he moved, his body, his face, the look in his eyes, and I pondered them fondly, almost like a lover. But my reveries would always end in depression. I knew neither his name nor where he came from. I tried to fathom why he had made such an impression on me, but I could not. Eventually, whenever his image loomed in my mind, I would expel it forcibly by throwing myself into work, storming around the wine-press, barking orders at the men, finding fault in all they did, and confusing them with my strangely erratic behavior.

Time passed, and the day of my wedding drew nearer. I tried to muster some enthusiasm for the event, but I could not. Martha would make a good wife. Although far from pretty, she was gentle and attentive, and perhaps later, after years of marriage with sons of my own, I might achieve a measure of contentment. But there was an aching hunger within me, which I knew could not be satisfied by family life.

And then one night, just as I was sitting down to my supper with my aunt and cousins, Lazarus arrived in a state of high excitement and begged me to come to his house. He refused to answer questions, only bade me come, but I could tell from his laughter and shining eyes that no disaster had occurred. My vexed aunt said that it could surely wait until I had eaten, but Lazarus was adamant, insisting that I come immediately, pulling me by the hand to the door. My curiosity was stronger than my hunger, so I went with him. It was a warm night, and he led me upstairs to the flat open roof of his house.

Emerging onto the roof-top, I saw a group of men reclining on cushions in a semi-circle, lit by the flickering glow of oil-lamps, their backs towards us. Martha moved silently among them, filling their cups with wine as they listened intently to the speaker around whom they were grouped. Before him, leaning on her elbow and gazing rapturously up at him lay a girl. It was Mary.

> *Ye have heard that it was said by them of old time,*
> *Thou shalt not commit adultery: But I say unto you,*
> *That whosoever looketh on a woman to lust after*
> *her hath committed adultery with her already in his*
> *heart*
> Matthew 5:27-28

I turned to Lazarus, amazed. He grinned and winked at me in mischievous joy, before beckoning silently to Martha, who came to join us in the doorway, her face glowing with happiness. We took cups from the tray and squatted in the shadows as I questioned them. They answered in whispers, not daring to break the concentration of the group. Mary had arrived that evening with the strangers, who had waited outside while she came into the house and prostrated herself before Lazarus, begging his forgiveness. He and Martha had naturally been astonished at her sudden appearance after so long an absence, but Lazarus's anger had melted as he listened to her story.

Mary had, indeed, become a prostitute after running away from home. She had left in a spirit of anger, frustration and revenge, jealous of the freedom men had which she felt she had an equal right to. For a time she believed she had gained it.

Equipped with the dual weapons of youth and beauty, she had soon gained highest status in the coven of raddled whores she had latched onto, and had the pick of the superiors among the platoon of Roman soldiers that they followed. Her charms had been fought over; a man had nearly been killed because of her; and Mary had experienced a sense of power over men she never dreamed could exist. Through introductions in Jerusalem she soon found herself in high society. A rich Jewish pimp had adopted her and established her in her own house in Magdala, a village near

Capernaum, with a cadre of regular wealthy customers, Roman and Jew, who kept her in a life of luxury and ease. Her presence was not popular, however, with the people of the village, particularly the Pharisees, who called profanities as they passed her dwelling, and would spit at her if she ventured into the street, threatening retribution for her harlotry.

Then one day a group of them had invaded her home and dragged her from the bed where she had been entertaining a rich merchant. Allowing her enough time to throw on a robe, they had dragged her out of the house by her hair and through the streets to the catcalls and jeers of women and children who stood to watch on their doorsteps. Her heart beating wildly with anger and fear, Mary had fought and scratched to no avail, until she was dumped, bruised and defeated, in a dusty square before a group of men sitting in the shade of a wall.

Uncertain of her fate, Mary kept her head bowed, staring at the ground under the shield of her unbound hair. Her angry captors harangued and accused in a babble of voices until they realized that none could be heard, and the din subsided, leaving one spokesman to state their case. He, in strident and indignant tone, declared that she was an adulteress who had been discovered in the very act of fornication. Was it not right that she should be stoned to death in accordance with the laws of Moses?

There was a silence, and Mary waited with expectant dread the first sharp blow of the thrown rocks that would leave her bloody and lifeless. A sob shook her body as she remembered the house in Bethany, her father, brother and sister, and the real love she had known from them, compared to the merely carnal lust of her clients.

The silence continued. She felt the answer to the question like a bowstring pulled tight before the agreed signal for release, but no signal came. Why did they wait before they condemned her? Shifting her eyes furtively up from the sanded cracks of the ground, she peered through the hanging curtain of her hair. A few feet in front of her she saw a man's finger moving in the dust. It seemed to be writing something. The strokes of the finger were slow and deliberate, with a languid quality that seemed at odds with the situation. Then he spoke. The tone was matter-of-fact, but the voice was strange, both commanding and questioning, authoritative yet gentle.

"He that is without sin among you—let him first cast a stone at her."

At this there were murmurs from the men, first of satisfaction that there was to be a stoning, but gradually changing to groans as it dawned on them, and Mary herself, that there was no man there, not even in the whole world, who could meet that requirement.

A muttering and a shuffling were followed by silence. After what seemed an age, Mary parted her hair and looked around her. Her accusers were gone. Before her, in the lengthening shadow of the wall, sat the stranger, slowly scribbling again in the sand, surrounded by his friends. Meeting her inquisitive glance, he asked if anyone condemned her. At first she could not answer. He seemed infinitely remote, sitting there so calmly. And his question went to her heart.

"Is there anyone here who condemns you?"

There was one. She condemned herself. The months of wanton debauchery flashed before her eyes, loveless and calculating, selfish and mercenary. The other accusers, the hypocrites, had fled, unable to face this stranger's challenge.

"No," she had breathed eventually.

"Then I do not condemn you either. Go, and sin no more." And with that he rose, his companions with him, and walked slowly away down one of the alleys that led off the square.

Without knowing what she was doing, but believing that it was the most important moment in her life, Mary was on her feet in an instant, running after the men, and throwing herself in the dust at her saviour's feet. She wept and repented, swearing to quit her life of harlotry and sin, groveling on the ground, clutching the man's feet, pleading with him to take her home.

Gentle hands reached down and lifted her up, and the man's

eyes looked into hers with a deep and unfathomable compassion. He asked her where she came from, and she sobbed out her story. When she had finished, he smiled and turned to his friends, asking if they were willing to return a lost lamb to its fold. They, too, had smiled and willingly acquiesced, and they set out that day for Bethany, two days' walk away.

On the way Mary never left her hero's side, listening enthralled to the things he said to his companions and to people he met on the road. He was a prophet, a teacher, and his message was unlike any she had heard before. By the time they reached Bethany, Mary was a devoted disciple. She poured out his message to Martha and Lazarus, who, skeptical at first, had also strongly warmed to the stranger when they had invited him in with his followers to give grateful thanks for the return of their prodigal sister.

And now, Lazarus said, I must meet him too. He was sure that I would be impressed. We stood up and Lazarus led me forward. As we stepped into the light, the talking stopped and all heads turned in our direction. My glance naturally fell on the man in the centre who had been speaking, and my heart leapt with sudden surprise. It was he! The man I had seen John baptize! The Master!

> *And Simon he surnamed Peter;*
> *And James the son of Zebedee, and John the brother of James; and he surnamed them Boanerges, which is, The sons of thunder:*
> *And Andrew, and Phillip, and Bartholomew; and Matthew, and Thomas, and James the son of Alphatus, and Thoddaeus, and Simon the Canaanite,*
> *And Judas Iscariot, which also betrayed him . . .*
> Mark 3:16-19

You must remember that night, Peter, for you were one of the visitors, along with John, James, Thomas, Matthew, and all the others, my dear brothers! But you may not have noticed the way I trembled as Lazarus brought me forward to introduce me. Oh, the feeling as if lightning had flashed through my blood when the Master rose and kissed me in welcome! He held me at arm's length and looked searchingly into my eyes before sitting me down at his left, and I learned all that I had yearned to know since seeing him in Bethabara: his name and lineage; what he preached and where he had traveled, and the followers he had gathered in his campaign; volunteers such as yourself, willing to give up their livelihoods and devote themselves entirely to him and the cause. I listened entranced as he spoke, my gaze never leaving his beautiful face.

All he said was new and exciting to me. He spoke of revolt, but not the violent kind nurtured by the hatred and bitterness that had burned for so long in my heart against our oppressors. His was a revolt of love, and of a complete transformation that must take place in the individual heart before a change in the world could come about. A voluntary rooting out of the weeds of evil from ones soul before the seeds of the Kingdom of God could he sown and flourish. He spoke with such conviction and authority, that I quickly became convinced. Hatred and evil bred more of the same and they could only be conquered by love. It was as simple as that. He spoke of a Kingdom of Goodness being established on earth, and all men living together in brotherhood and peace. No more wars. No more strife. No more poverty.

Martha, leaning down to pour me wine, whispered shyly that it appeared I had fallen under his spell like Mary. It was indeed as if he had cast magic with his words. And if she and I and these other men had fallen, why should not countless others do likewise, with hearts lit by a new and burning hope for the future?

It grew late, and one by one the Master's men removed themselves from the group and found themselves a space to sleep, but I lingered, hypnotized by his words and personality, until only he, Mary, and I were left.

Eventually I dared to speak, having made up my mind. I asked him, begged him, to allow me to come along with him on his mission. Nothing seemed more important in the world. If rejected, my life would be an empty desert. He looked at me, the light of the flickering oil-lamp dancing in his eyes, and asked if I was a good man. I replied that I was a miserable sinner, but I believed in him, and was prepared to devote my life to the spreading of his teaching. He smiled and said that theirs was a life of poverty and toil, long journeys and often days without food or rest. Would I be prepared to endure that for his sake, without losing hope? I said I would, and a thousand times more, if he would only accept me as one of his men.

The smile faded from his lips, and a frown furrowed his brow. Another disciple would bring the number to twelve, and that would be enough, but, he said, he had chosen the others himself, and now here was one who was choosing him. Yet he would accept me, for he had the feeling that I was one who would do him great service in the future. He leant forward and kissed me on both cheeks, calling me "Brother Judas", and informing me that they were to set off early the next morning, and that I was one of them.

He rose, and after gently extricating his hand from Mary's quick, pleading grasp, found the place where John lay, and curled up beside him under a cloak, against the chill of the early morning air.

Hardly able to believe my happiness, I went to seek Martha and Lazarus, leaving Mary, her head bowed, beside the dying lamp.

I found them talking quietly at the foot of the stairs and told them my glorious news. They were almost as excited as I was, but not surprised. Lazarus hugged me, laughing, saying that he, too, would have volunteered, but believing that I was more worthy to fill vacant place, he had held back to give me the opportunity to offer myself. Martha smiled wistfully and kissed me on the cheek, saying that she was proud for me, and that the mission was far more important than our marriage. If all went well, it would not be long before we became man and wife in the Kingdom of God, and how much more wonderful that would be!

I bade them goodnight and returned home, waking my bewildered aunt and cousins to kiss them farewell and choose what to take with me. In the end I decided merely to change into plainer garb and take a purse stuffed with coins. A few hours were left before dawn but my excitement would not let me sleep, and I was impatiently ready when the sun rose to begin to play my own role in the great coming drama of awakening the people to the Kingdom.

> *... blind Bartmaeus, the son of Timaeus, sat by the highway side begging ...*
> Mark 10:46

The exultant joy I felt as we set off in the morning was enormous; a physical sensation of boundless inextinguishable delight seemed to flood my being. Looking back from crest of the hill I could see the tiny figures of Lazarus, Martha and Mary still watching and waving from their doorway. Tears came to my eyes. Not tears of sorrow or regret, but tears of pride. It seemed that my life had been meaningless until then. Now I had something to believe in, someone to live for. I belonged to the Master, and I would do everything within my power to serve him well. Turning my back on Bethany, I hurried to catch up with the ambling group of men, now my brothers, on the road to Capernaum.

Need I speak of our travels with the Master, Peter? You were there when he preached to the crowds great and small along the way. You saw the dawning expressions of hope on the faces of those that accepted and believed in his message. We shared the glory as well as the scorn and derision and more than occasional hungry nights with the open fields for our beds and stones to pillow our heads.

The brothers all looked at the Master through different eyes, and none of us really knew what to expect of him. I suspect that you, Peter, would have preferred him to be more aggressive, a conqueror Christ you would have gladly championed with a sword. James and John seemed more interested in the imagined power and glory they would inherit when the Master established his Kingdom. And several of the others seemed not to understand him at all. I sometimes wondered why he had chosen them; they were so simple and uneducated, though innocent and good-hearted.

You were my favourite among the brothers, Peter, honest enough to admit when you did not understand, and asked for explanation without fear of rebuke. And you were the only one interested in bettering yourself by learning to read, with Matthew and me as your teachers, when we had time at rest by the roadside while the Master was at prayer. You were a slow but dogged student, and made enough progress for me to be confident that you understand all that I confide to you in this epistle.

If I had to criticize anything about the behavior of the Master towards us, I would probably single out the favor he seemed to show John over the rest of us. I don't see why he should have had the place at the Master' right at meal times and be fed with the choicest morsels by his own hand, and why he was always chosen as his sleeping partner on cold nights when we needed another human body for warmth. Admittedly, John was the youngest, but in my opinion the attention was not good for him, causing him to be spoiled and smug rather than honored and blessed. I fought to quell my jealousy, but it was difficult.

Jealousy is a deadly sin. Pride is too, but it is a far more pleasurable sensation, and I swelled with it when the Master made me the keeper of the communal purse. Admittedly, most of the money in it was that which I had brought along with me, but that didn't matter. It made me feel important and gave me an identity in the group. Any recognition by the Master, however small, was like manna from Heaven to me. If anything was needed, it was I who would dole out the coins and note down the expenditure. I was surprised that Matthew, who was more used to working with money, had not been chosen, but I was pleased.

Although I have never been in love, I can only imagine that my feeling for the Master must have been something comparable to that particular condition. To serve him, to please him, to promote him, was my sole aim and intention. I wanted to share him with the world, for every one living to learn from his example and teaching. Words of scorn and rejection from cynical listeners would make me feel actually physically ill. He was the King – sent by God, and I wanted everyone to know it.

But somehow, something was missing. Something special was needed to blaze his name abroad. We occasionally heard stories of other itinerant preachers who cast out demons and performed wondrous deeds. But whenever dissatisfied listeners interrupted the Master and demanded a sign to prove that he was a true prophet, he would rebuke them. It was a godless generation that demanded signs and miracles, he said, like children at a circus. The greatest miracle, if they wished to call it that, would be the unhardening of their hearts and their welcoming in of the Kingdom. He was right of course. But nevertheless, I couldn't help feeling that even just the tiniest of miracles wouldn't do our cause any harm.

And so, when the Master eventually sent each of us out on our own individual preaching tours, and I had finished delivering the word to a small gathering in a village square, around a well, or even in a tavern, I deliberately did not disabuse those who asked if it was really true that the Master could make the blind see, the deaf hear, and raise the dead to life, but replied in the affirmative. It wasn't my fault if they were too stupid to understand metaphors. They would go away happy, many of them voluntarily baptized, passing on the stories they had heard, elaborating them out of all proportion, until it would seem the Master was the greatest miracle worker of all time. I didn't care. His fame was being spread and the great coming liberation was being preached.

The final venue of my particular tour ended in Jericho, but, being a busy trading town, I found it difficult to command attention in the bustling market square, and was even ordered to move on by irritable stallholders when I tried to gather a crowd. Instead, I found myself at the city gates with a small captive audience of paupers who sat in the shade begging alms from the merchants passing in and out with their camel trains and laden donkeys.

Squatting before this motley crew, I related to them the glory of the Kingdom to come, omitting references to blindness, deafness or dumbness, since most of them suffered from one or more of those afflictions. Instead, I presented to them the idea of a world without hunger or poverty, where all men were equal, where no one would be homeless or friendless; a world without kings, tyrants or taxes, the wealth shared by all the people, and where the only law was love. Tears sprang to my eyes at my eloquence, and neither was my audience unmoved, showing their appreciation with murmurs and muttered amens. Some said that it sounded like a dream, but I assured them that it could all be possible if they would only banish sin from their hearts and accept the Master as their Deliverer.

"I would like to see this Master of yours," called a voice, and turning, I saw that it came from an old blind man seated next to an armless mute. Suppressing the impulse to answer that it might be rather difficult in his case, I informed them that the Master would in fact be visiting their city before too long, and until he did, they should bear all I had told them in mind. Then, thanking them for their attention, I rose and set off on my return to Capernaum.

My preaching mission accomplished, I was eager to get back to the Master as soon as possible, but after only a short walk from Jericho I felt tired, and tempted by the cooling shade of an orchard of fig-trees which sheltered a glittering pond, I entered. After slaking my thirst, I curled up under some bushes and fell asleep.

I woke suddenly some time later, disturbed by a sound. Raising the scarf from my eyes, I peered in the direction from where it had come. The lowering sun now gilded the grove with a soft golden light, and the figure of a man was approaching the pool, dry twigs snapping under his feet, the sounds of which had woken me. He trailed a staff casually behind him, and as he got closer I recognized him as the blind man I had spoken to at the gates of Jericho. I was surprised at the sureness of his footing. It was almost as though he could see.

I soon discovered that in fact he could, although he did not see me, concealed as I was by the bushes. He sat down by the pool and, opening a grubby handkerchief, took out and slowly counted the handful of coins he had earned from that day's begging. Satisfied, he re-wrapped them, stood up and began to undress for a dip in the water. I watched the old rascal indignantly. Day after day he sat there at the city gates playing on the sympathy of gullible passers-by, and making a most dishonest daily bread. But his sightless stare was most certainly convincing. Even I had been taken in!

As he entered the pool, leaving his clothes and money behind on the bank, I decided to teach him a lesson. He waded out in the water, his back towards me. I crept cautiously out of the bushes, snatched his discarded things and quickly returned to my hiding place.

After wallowing for a while and wiping the grime from his body, he turned and made his way back to the bank, but before getting there he stopped and stared in amazement at the vacant spot where his clothes had been. He looked around, an expression of terror on his face, then called out, asking if anyone was there. I kept silent for a few minutes, enjoying his plight and giving him time to become more frantic in his cries, before emerging from the bushes with his things in my hand. It was clear that he saw and recognized me instantly, although he averted his gaze and assumed the customary blank stare. I asked him what the trouble was, and turning his sightless eyes in my direction, he replied that someone had stolen his clothes, and would I please help a poor blind man? I told him to forget the pretence and began to upbraid him for his parasitic existence, threatening to expose him to the authorities, and demanding an explanation for his abominable behavior. Eventually, with a sigh of resignation, be said that he would explain all if I would only return his clothes and money. I agreed to his bargain and, after he had dressed, we sat on the bank of the pool and he told me his story.

His name was Bartimaeus—more commonly known as "Blind Bartimaeus". Born to a crippled beggar and an alcoholic prostitute, his life had been hopeless from the outset. The family money had trickled in from begging and whoring: enough for supper, drink, and the seediest of lodgings, and there had been no thought of teaching him a trade. His father, recognizing the potential sympathy-value of a fresh young innocent, had taught the young Bartimaeus the art of rolling his eyeballs back inside his head, so that it appeared to anyone else that he was nothing less than totally blind. This he had perfected so well that he had become the chief breadwinner of the family, and after his mother had drunk herself to death, his father had taken the child from city to city, where they had crouched pathetically on the steps of synagogue and temple, reaping in coin the pity of those who passed in and out. Eventually his father had died, and Bartimaeus, used to the routine by that time, had come to the conclusion that he was not fit for any other profession. He had chosen Jericho as his ideal pitch, Jerusalem being too big, with too much competition; and there he had settled, appearing every morning at his usual place at the gate, returning to his hovel on the outskirts every evening. I was the first person ever to catch him out.

He pleaded with me to keep his secret. He was a poor man and could give nothing to pledge my silence, only rely on the goodness of my heart. He was in my power.

I asked what he thought about the message I had preached at the city gates, and he replied that the Kingdom of God sounded wonderful, but it would be impossible to establish in this world, men being too desperately selfish to care about the wellbeing of others. I told him that it was because they had no idea or hope, and had not been shown the sublime alternative that the Master offered—which Bartimaeus must now reveal to them.

That was my condition for not revealing his fraud. He could continue his sordid, lying life, eking out his pittance at the Jericho gates, but he must at the same time be baptized as a believer by me in the pool, and henceforth preach the message of the Master tirelessly, telling of the marvelous things he had done and would do for the people if they would only repent and strive to establish God's Kingdom on Earth.

He wept and blessed me, kissing my hands and swearing to do as I said. I warned him that I would return to Jericho when he least expected it, and if I found that he had not been doing as I ordered I would announce his deception immediately, and he would probably be stoned to death by all those he had cheated. Again he swore, and after his baptism I gave him a few coins before setting off again on the road to Capernaum and my beloved Master, my heart glowing with my accomplishment, the shouted blessings of Bartimaeus fading behind me in the distance.

> *For this people's heart is waxed gross, and their ears are dull of hearing, and their eyes they have closed; lest at anytime they should see with their eyes, and hear with their ears, and should understand with their heart, and should be converted, and I should heal them.*
> Matthew 13:15

Within a few days we were all together again, returned from our lone preaching missions and united around the Master. How eagerly we listened to each other's adventures, and accounts of the hospitality we had or had not been shown. We had been out in the fields scattering the seeds, the Master told us, and soon would come the time when we would go out and gather the glorious harvest.

How proud we all were of our work, although perhaps secretly unsure of just how much we had accomplished. The message had appealed to the poor and downtrodden, who had all to gain from the promised New World order, but the proud and wealthy had been generally scornful. Strict Pharisees had talked of blasphemy, and the Sadducees totally dismissive. In a country so divided, what would be the outcome of our harvest? And even if it were bountiful, what would be the reaction of our overlords, the Romans to the budding revolution we were encouraging? Such questions we dared not ask aloud, but still they remained, and no matter how we tried to ignore them, we knew that one day they would have to be faced and answered.

When we later retraced the steps of our individual journeys in the company of the Master, we found that our words, like seeds indeed, had taken root however feebly, and in villages and small towns on our itinerary curious crowds turned up to hear him speak. News of the Master had spread, and those who came were eager to witness this possible Messiah in person, whether they believed in him or not. Our congregations were made up, on the whole, of the poor and ignorant, many bringing with them ill and handicapped members of their families in the vain hope that the tales of miraculous cures of which they had heard could be performed on them. Along with them came devout Pharisees, jealous and suspicious of the Master's teaching, eager to trap him in questions on the laws of Moses, in which he might betray himself as the charlatan they presumed him to be. None were successful. The Master spoke in simple parables and stories, which the crowds, whether they understood them or not, at least found entertaining, a far cry from the obscure, humorless cant they were used to hearing from their religious leaders. They would wonder and applaud when the Master, in answer to the cunning questions of the Pharisees, with admirable simplicity made them fall into their traps with his own questions, leaving them squirming and speechless. And then with amazed incredulity they would listen as he condemned them as outright hypocrites who demanded conduct from others which they themselves had never followed. Shamefaced and furious, they would retaliate by accusing him either of drunkenness, consorting with sinners or collaboration with the Devil. But all their accusations were as weak as water, and they would depart in defeat, allowing the Master to use their behavior as yet another lesson for us to learn by.

He worked wonders with his words, and many came afterwards to be baptized in his name, but I could not help noticing the disappointed expressions on the faces of those who had brought their sick to be healed. At least one miracle was needed to cement the stone of the Kingdom firmly into its foundation.

And so it was, as we were nearing Jericho, having stirred interest mild and great along the way, that an idea came to me. If a miracle was really necessary, then I had one made to order! Absurdly simple, yet completely foolproof! My brow prickled with sweat as it hatched in my brain. I had to do it! Whatever the results, I must at least try. Using the excuse that I was going ahead to find suitable lodgings, I hurried off, planning it all out as I went.

Jericho was soon in sight, and I was in the shade of the lofty gate where the beggars sat crying mournfully to the passing merchants. Spotting Bartimaeus, I made my way towards him, ignoring the greetings of those who recognized me. Crouching beside him and grasping his arm, I told him I had come. His face grew ashen and he stammered out that he had done as I ordered. Every day he talked of the Master and the promised Kingdom. If I did not believe him, I had only to ask the other beggars. They were sick of hearing about it and laughed when he arrived in the morning, calling him "Bartimaeus the Prophet". I told him to be quiet, and whispered my plan into his ear.

At first he was incredulous and protested, but I reminded him that he had no choice in the matter, and warned him that if he did not do as I said I would certainly expose him. At this he fell mute and I related my plan again, making him repeat certain details to make sure that there would be no mistake. Satisfied, I told him to remain alert and await our imminent arrival. As a final incentive I thrust a handful of coins from the purse into his hand before rising to hurry back to the Master and my advancing brothers.

Thankfully you were still some distance from the city when I greeted you, breathlessly muttering my apologies. Then, by stumbling strategies, I managed to fall in step beside the Master. Glancing up at the profile of his calm, resolute face, I was almost afraid to speak, but summoning up my courage, I did. I told him that at the gates of Jericho there was a crowd of wretched beggars. One of them, a blind man, would call out to him in the name of David, in recognition of his lineage, and ask to be cured. The Master need only touch his eyes. It would be enough. Would he do it?

He turned and looked at me searchingly without losing his stride. I asked him to trust me, my soul squirming under his all-seeing gaze. Would he do it? Simply touch the blind man's eyes?

With a slight raise of his brow, his eyes left mine, and wordlessly we continued forward, I confused and unsure.

The city gates appeared, and as we approached, the people around them, entering and leaving, stopped to stare at us. We must have presented a curious sight, a little army of thirteen men striding purposefully towards Jericho without animals or merchandise.

As we were about to enter, people parted to let us pass and a low murmur of curiosity arose, broken suddenly by the cry I had been waiting for.

"Son of David—have mercy on me!"

It was Blind Bartimeus. The Master stopped, and we with him. Again the cry came. Some of the crowd tried to silence Bartimaeus with angry words, but the Master asked for him to be brought forward. I hurried to where he was and led him to the Master, who asked what he wanted of him. Bartimaeus replied that he wanted to see.

After a pause, during which I hardly dared breathe, the Master inexplicably knelt down and spat in the dust of the road. Then, mixing it into a paste with his fingers, he stood up and wiped the mixture on Bartimeus's eyelids. He told him to bathe his eyes in water. Spying an animal trough nearby, I led him to it and, dipping his hands into the water, he put them to his eyes. Almost immediately he began to jump about rejoicing, exclaiming at the top of his voice that he could see! He could see!

And indeed, the pupils had returned to his formerly opaque eyeballs as he went around touching things and staring wonderingly into the faces of all around him, viciously into mine. Our first miracle had been performed.

At first the onlookers were dumbfounded, thunder-struck. But then they gradually found their tongues, and their voices rose in an excited babble. The news spread like wildfire and more people hurried from within the city, cramming the gateway. Other beggars, blind or limbless, shuffled forward, entreating the Master to cure them also, only to be trampled under the feet of their healthier brothers, who advanced begging for miracles less physical—wealth, success, beauty, power. Some of them grasped at his clothing, claiming him for their individual needs and fighting off those behind them, until the situation was out of hand.

    Throwing an exasperated look at me, the Master managed to tear himself away and retreat in haste from the unentered city, protected by his men, who threatened blows to those who followed pleading for a great distance. I was elated. My plan had succeeded. Thanks to me, the fame of the Master would increase a hundredfold!

> *Then saith the woman of Samaria unto him, How is it that thou, being a Jew, askest drink of me, which am a woman of Samaria? for the Jews have no dealings with the Samaritans.*
> John 4:9

Not only did the incident help to spread the Master's reputation as a miraculous healer throughout the land, but it also increased his standing in the eyes of you and the brothers. I remember your amazed questions as to how he could have managed to restore the sight of a blind man, and his reply that all things were possible with God's help. He told you to concentrate on the spiritual rather than the physical, and stressed that the miracle we were hoping to bring about was the establishment of the Kingdom of God.

Nevertheless, you had been deeply impressed. And although I never mentioned the incident to the Master, or he to me, I nursed a glowing pride for what I had done. Buoyed by the success of Bartimaeus's "cure", I kept my eyes peeled for the chance of topping it and bringing the Master even greater glory. In Samaria I found the opportunity I had been looking for.

You won't have forgotten that time, Peter. It was when we left the Master to rest by a well while we went to buy food in a nearby village, and found him talking to a woman when we returned, who called him Christ, and ran to fetch her neighbours to meet him. God knows what they had been talking about. We were perhaps too embarrassed to ask, she being a woman and a Samaritan to boot. But she was certainly excited, and returned with other villagers who entreated him to stay with them for a while as a guest, to which the Master agreed, although several of the brothers were reluctant to break bread with Samaritans.

But we did stay, and late in the evening, after the Master had preached to one of our most attentive and receptive audiences and we had been well fed and royally entertained, I stayed up talking with the Samaritan woman alone, after you had all bedded down for the night.

We sat together chatting quietly as we shared a final flagon of wine under the hanging vine of her terrace. From inside came the faint snores of her husband. She confessed that they were not officially married. She had lived with several men in her time, and this one would probably not be the last. She was a vivacious, romantic woman, a trifle coarse and cheap with her shiny bracelets and rings, but honest and direct, and I liked her. She asked me about my own love-life without coyness, but with a flirtatiousness in her eyes that suggested nothing would be amiss if we were to share a few stolen moments of love together.

I answered that my life was now totally devoted to the Master. There was a girl waiting for me in Bethany, and some day, when the Master's mission was fulfilled, I would return and marry her. She nodded with a smile, saying that the Master was a special man. I was wise to devote my attention to him. She believed that he would accomplish great things.

She asked about Martha. Was she frigid? Had I found it hard to win her? I replied that she was a virgin, and very shy, rather than cold. The Samaritan woman laughed and said that she had a remedy that could ensure I had a memorable wedding night. I asked her what she meant.

Looking at me boldly, she told me that she had a reputation as a witch in her village, although she was nothing of the sort. She merely knew how to distill the essence of herbs and flowers that she collected from the nearby hills, and could make them into potions and medicines. The secret art had been passed on by her grandmother, who had died some years before. One of her specialties was an essence, which added to the cup of a bride on her wedding day would ensure the loss of all inhibitions and a night of bliss undreamed of by the wildest lecher. It worked even on the most timorous of virgins. I was welcome to a phial as a wedding present. Declining graciously, I asked her what other concoctions she produced. She rose and took the oil-lamp, beckoning me to bring the wine pitcher and follow her.

We went into the house and she unlocked a door at the end of a passage. Setting the lamp on a bench, she pointed to some shelves against the wall where rows of bottles, jars and tubes filled with coloured liquid gleamed like diluted jewels, and announced that some of them were worth their weight in gold. Taking down a small flask of what looked like milk, she told me it was the aphrodisiac she had already mentioned. She could not count the number of grateful satisfied husbands who had returned her such profuse thanks after their wedding nights. Then, with a raised eyebrow, she held out a container of amber liquid, saying that perhaps it might be more suitable for me. It guaranteed an unflagging nightlong erection. I laughed and shook my head, refilling her cup with wine to hide my embarrassment. Pointing to a translucent red liquid, I asked what it was for.

She turned back to her potions and began to describe their properties. The ruby was to rid the womb of an unwanted child. It always caused her sorrow to be asked for that one, but if it were the final decision of an unfortunate mother who could not cope with another hungry mouth to feed, she would concur. And to prevent its further need, she usually recommended the emerald liquid, which caused permanent barrenness. Or, if preferred, the sapphire juice next to it which would render sterile the seed of the husband. For childless couples, the violet potion, drunk together, greatly increased their chances of creating a baby.

I asked if all her handiwork concerned sex and procreation, and she laughed, saying they were the ones most in demand, but there were all kinds of remedies and drugs. She rattled them off in a list. There was one to prevent drunkenness; one to prevent baldness; one to induce bliss and ecstasy; one to improve sight; one to cause loss of weight; one, an untraceable poison, which killed instantly; one to render a person into a death-like trance; one to restore memory; one to suppress pain . . .

I stopped her, and pointed to a bottle of cloudy yellow liquid, asking her to repeat what it would do. She said that a sip of it was enough to send anyone into a deep coma, without traceable heartbeat, pulse or breath, and even the most skilled of doctors would conclude that death had taken place. But the effect wore off after three days and the person woke as if from a dream, without the slightest harm whatever.

I stared at the liquid, wondering why I had found the idea of it more fascinating than the others. I asked if she was certain that it worked, and she replied that apart from having tested it on various animals, there was a girl living in a nearby village who was living proof of its effectiveness. In love with a young man her parents disapproved of, and commanded by them to marry one of their choice that she hated, she had come to the woman and purchased the potion. On the eve of her wedding, alone in her chamber, she had drunk the liquid and seemingly died. The wedding feast had become a funeral, and after a day's mourning by her grief-stricken family she had been entombed. Her lover then, as they had secretly arranged together, stole her unconscious body from the grave under cover of darkness and transported it to his own village, and she had married him there as soon as she had recovered. If I didn't believe it she could take me to the village and introduce the happy couple. They already had three children, with another on the way!

I replied that it would not be necessary. I believed and trusted her. Then I reminded her that she had offered me a wedding present. She laughed and asked which it was to be? For the use of the bride or the groom? The bridegroom, I answered.

She smirked and held out the milky white liquid, but I refused it and demanded the cloudy yellow. She looked surprised, but I said it was the one I wanted and asked her to give it to me as promised, without any questions. With an indifferent shrug, she poured out a measure into a small phial, and handed it over, warning me to be careful. Promising I would, I offered her money, but she waved it away with a yawn.

We returned to the terrace, but after a last drink she bade me goodnight and went inside to join her snoring man, leaving me to try to understand exactly why I had chosen to take this strange drug from the woman.

And then with a sudden shock that made me catch my breath, the idea was formed and understood. Until then, the Master's reputation was known only in Galilee and Samaria, but this new plan of mine, if accomplished, could rock Judea to its roots and spread his name through the streets of even the holy city itself. Trembling with excitement, I put together the pieces of the scheme. It had to be foolproof.

Then I rose, gazing at the stars. It was after midnight. If I set out immediately I could be at my destination within a few hours, be able to explain my plan and have it either accepted or rejected, and be back in Samaria by mid-afternoon. There was no time for consultation with the Master. I felt that I must act at that moment while the inspiration still burned in my brain. Placing the little phial of precious liquid inside my shirt and hugging it there, I strode off without hesitation on the moonlit path to Bethany.

> *Now a certain man was sick, named Lazarus, of Bethany, the town of Mary and her sister Martha. (It was that Mary which anointed the Lord with ointment, and wiped his feet with her hair, whose brother Lazarus was sick.) Therefore his sisters sent unto him, saying, Lord, behold, he whom thou lovest is sick.*
> John 11:1-3

I arrived in Bethany soon after daybreak and made my way straight to Lazarus's house by a route avoiding my aunt and cousins place. There was no time for socializing. I was on a serious mission.

Some workers, already turning the olive-press in the yard as I entered, offered me a sleepy "good morning" as though I had never been away. I climbed the steps to the roof and found Lazarus, Martha and Mary at breakfast. They rose and embraced me with cries of astonished welcome, bidding me sit down and eat with them, which I did with a will, for I was fiercely hungry after my long journey. While I ate they filled me in with all that had happened since I left. I learned that business was good, my cousins' wine was selling well, there had been a wedding, a couple of deaths, and number of babies had been born. But what about me? What adventures had I been through since setting out on the great quest for human souls? They thirsted for knowledge of the Master's progress.

I told them all about our travels, of things the Master had said and done, and they listened eagerly, particularly Mary, whom seemed a different woman. She was as beautiful as ever, but the sullenness had vanished, and her eyes shone with the innocence of a child as she leaned forward, hanging on my every word.

Cautiously, I related the 'cure' that the Master had performed on Blind Bartimaeus at my instigation, and the reaction of the crowd who had witnessed it. I asked if they censured me for fabricating such a deceit, but on the contrary, Lazarus laughed heartily, saying that it was a splendid joke, and Martha, patting my hand reassuringly, said that I had cleverly taken advantage of a chance to increase the Master's fame. Mary was not as quick with praise and asked if I had thought it really necessary to add this element of sensationalism. I replied vehemently that I had, for I was determined that the Master should become peerless as quickly as possible, and I would seize every opportunity for making him so. Martha applauded my words, Lazarus clapped me on the back, and Mary glanced at me with a look of guarded admiration. I knew that then was the moment to lay the plan before them.

Warily, but with more confidence, I asked that if they had the opportunity to fabricate a miracle, untrue, yet unchallengeable, one which would help to spread the name and fame of the Master far and wide, would they reject or accept the chance? Unanimously, they said that they would take it.

And so, my hand trembling a little with excitement, I reached inside my shirt and brought out the little container of cloudy yellow liquid. Holding it out, I said that their words were brave, but were they prepared to put them to the proof? Puzzled, they asked me to explain.

I handed over the phial and they inspected it while I told them about the deathlike effect that the liquid had on whoever drank it, of the woman who had made it and the proofs she had offered me. Still puzzled, Lazarus asked what it had to do with them. After looking around to check that we were completely alone, I related my plan as simply and straightforwardly as I could.

Suppose Lazarus was to suddenly fall ill and die? Martha and Mary, greatly distraught, would inform the rest of the village who would come to pay their last respects; doctors and rabbis would confirm the death, and after anointing the body would be entombed. The ritual mourning would continue, with friends and relatives offering condolences, filling the house with sorrow. But suppose then that on the third day the Master should arrive? And suppose, on hearing of the death of Lazarus, he should go out to the tomb, order the stone to be rolled aside, and call Lazarus to come forth and return to life? And suppose that Lazarus did as he was ordered? Could they imagine the confusion, the amazement, the incredible sensation that such an event would cause? I rocked the phial slowly in my hand, gazing at the revolving yellow liquid.

There was a stunned silence, and I knew that it was understood. Then all began to speak at once, Lazarus asking when it should be done, Martha wondering if I was positive as to the effects, and Mary asking if the Master had been informed of the plan.

I answered Mary's question first, replying that when one gave a gift, or performed a kind service for someone, one did not usually announce it beforehand and spoil the pleasant surprise. I reminded her of the Master's words on charity, of not letting the right hand know what the left was doing. My explanation seemed to satisfy her, for she remained silent.

To Martha I replied that I had not witnessed positive proofs of the effects of the drug, but I had an instinctive trust in the woman who had made it, even though she was a Samaritan. She, too, admired the Master and wished no harm to his followers. I would be back in the Samarian village that evening, and having informed him of the plan, the Master would be there at the end of three days, when the effects would have worn off. We must trust in God.

And to Lazarus I said that we must set things in motion almost immediately. As soon as I had left he must pretend to be unwell, and Martha and Mary should spread the news of his illness to neighbours. Then, that very night, he should take the potion, so that he would be "dead" by the early hours of the next morning.

I admitted that I had presented them with a sudden drastic disruption in their lives and wondered if they were they strong enough to face the strain of the tremendous attention the miracle would bring about?

They looked at each other in silence. Martha and Mary said that they would, but they were worried about Lazarus, for the burden of the task lay upon his shoulders. He replied that on the contrary, the hardest role would be theirs. He would be merely having a nice long sleep, while before them lay days of dramatic weeping and wailing and tearing of hair.

Suddenly we were all laughing and embracing each other, bound closer together in our conspiracy. We planned the events in detail. Lazarus's illness would be unspecific—a fever, a pain inside. Martha would be the one to discover his body in the morning. The empty phial must be disposed of. Mary would scream news of the death from the rooftop, which would bring the neighbours running. The empty cave in the cliff at the end of the garden would be the tomb, a purpose for which it had already been prepared. No one but Martha and Mary should anoint the body for interment. The winding sheets should be tied loosely. These and other things we discussed long into the morning, and I coached them in how they should behave when I arrived on the third day with the Master and his men.

Noon came; time for me to return to the Master. With bread, dates and wine to refresh me on the way, I wished them courage in their task, and set off for Samaria, turning again on the brink of the hill to see their tiny figures waving from the rooftop.

When I arrived at the Samaritan woman's house in the late afternoon, I discovered to my horror that the Master was no longer there! When I asked where he had gone, the woman merely shrugged. After they had woken and breakfasted, they had noticed my absence but decided to go on without me. I was welcome to stay for supper, she said.

I begged her to rack her brains for any mention of a destination. She thought for a moment, and then ventured that there had been some talk of a wedding in Cana. I turned and set off in that direction at once, ignoring her invitation for me to tarry until the morrow, before joining them. It would take me several hours to reach Cana, and darkness was already falling. I had no time to stop and explain why time was so precious. I had to find the Master and let him know what was happening as soon as possible. It was a matter of life or death!

*And the third day there was a marriage in Cana of
Galilee; and the mother of Jesus was there:
And both Jesus was called, and his disciples,
to the marriage.*
John 2:1-2

It was late by the time I reached Cana, well after midnight, judging by the moon and stars. My legs were ached, for I had made great haste, worried about the events that I had set in progress in Bethany.

The village was quiet and dark as I came down the hillside, apart from one house that was brightly lit, alive with the sound of music and laughter. I made my way towards it and, looking in through the gateway, saw a wedding party going on in the courtyard, which was lit by many lanterns and flickering candles, the air perfumed with smoking incense. Servants bearing flagons of wine and trays of sweetmeats passed among the chattering guests and the floor was strewn with flowers and green leaves. At the far end a group of men were making music with flutes, bells and drums, and a circle of onlookers surrounded a pair of dancers, encouraging them with rhythmic handclaps.

I entered and made my way through the merrymakers towards the circle. With huge relief I recognized somebody. It was Thomas. Then I noticed others, you among them, Peter, and knew that I was back again in the fold. Joining in the clapping, I saw with a shock that one of the dancers was the Master, and the other a woman.

She was not young, the hair under her black kerchief gray, but a beauty shone from her eyes as they gazed into those of the Master. They circled one another as they danced, with arms outstretched, fingers clicking and bodies swaying to the drumbeat.

The woman's movements were somewhat clumsy, as though not used to dancing, but the Master had picked up the rhythm and moved to it expertly, a smile of huge enjoyment on his face. It disturbed me to see a man and woman dancing together, but the circle seemed to see no wrong, laughing and singing as they clapped.

Eventually the Master and the woman ended their dance and left the floor to great applause, their places taken by James and John, who changed the pace of the music by whooping and whirling and wildly stamping their feet.

I went in search of the Master and found him sitting on some steps with a cup of wine in his hand, the woman by his side. He greeted my approach mockingly, addressing me as 'the prodigal returned'. I muttered my apologies, but he merely laughed. He was in a festive mood and offered me his cup, which I drank from eagerly, not only because I was thirsty from my long journey, but also because his lips had touched it.

Indicating the woman at his side, he introduced her to me as his mother, Mary. A surge of both relief and reverence rushed through me and, seizing her hand, I kissed and pressed it to my forehead. She pulled it away gently and modestly, thanking me for my respects. She smiled, but the lines etched on her face told of past pain and sorrow.

Remembering my urgent mission, I whispered to the Master that I had a very serious matter to discuss with him, but he shook his head, saying that it was not the time for seriousness. We were at a wedding feast, a time for gaiety and enjoyment. And bidding his mother take her ease, he led me by the hand back to the circle, pulled me into it, and we danced together to the clapping and encouragement of the onlookers.

I forced a smile onto my face. Everyone around me was happy, their minds on the wedding. Mine, however, was on a funeral. The pleasure of being chosen to dance with the Master was overshadowed by the dread of what may happen if I delayed too long in telling him what I had set in motion. I realized, though, that it would be impossible to broach the subject that night.

As pale dawn crept across the sky, the party guests began to retire. Those who lived in the village made their sleepy ways home to the calls of waking cockerels announcing the day—but the party was far from over. It would begin again in the early evening after all had been refreshed by sleep. Guests who had come from afar remained and bedded down wherever they could find space.

Tired though I was, I could not entertain the thought of sleep. Eagle-eyed, I watched the Master as he found a place under the palm trees in the centre of the courtyard. After fashioning pillows from the fallen leaves, he lay down beside his mother and closed his eyes. Soon the whole courtyard was littered with bodies, as though a peaceful, bloodless massacre had taken place.

When certain that most were sound asleep, I crept to the Master's side and gently shook his shoulder. His eyes opened slowly and blearily, and in a sleepy voice he asked what I wanted. I whispered that Lazarus was seriously ill, perhaps even dying, and wished to see him. His eyes half closed, he asked who Lazarus was. I reminded him of Mary, the adulteress he had saved in Magdala, and how he had returned her to her brother Lazarus in Bethany, where he and I had first met. He grunted in recognition, saying that Bethany was quite a walk away. There were still two nights of the wedding party left, but perhaps a visit to Lazarus might be considered when it was over. Then, shutting his eyes again and telling me not to worry, he drifted off into sleep.

An image of Lazarus, awakened in his shroud, scratching frantically against the stone of his tomb flashed into my head, and I shook the Master more urgently. He opened his eyes indignantly this time and asked me what I was about. There was nothing I could do but whisper carefully into his ear the miracle that I had prepared for him to accomplish. When I had finished he sat up abruptly, wide-awake, with a loud exclamation. Some sleepers around us reacted to his shout by turning over, but none of them awoke, and I hushed him to be quiet.

Beckoning for him to follow, I moved to the gateway of the courtyard and stepped outside, where the rising sun painted the houses of the village in a soft golden light. Within a few moments the Master was with me. He demanded angrily that I repeat my story, and I did, filling in more details of the plan. I emphasized that we must be in Bethany within two days or Lazarus's life would truly be in danger if he were locked any longer in the tomb.

The Master's face was grim as he listened to my tale. When I had finished, he began to admonish me in a stern, indignant voice for all that I had done, saying that it was a foolish and dangerous idea, and he wondered how I had dared to put it into practice without consulting him. What was I trying to make of him? A circus conjuror? A performer of tricks for the delight of ignorant sensation-seekers? They were not the kind of followers he sought. He wanted those who accepted his message of the Kingdom and acted to bring it about without being influenced by cheap wonders. I had done a great wrong.

I apologized and begged his forgiveness, but implored him to release Lazarus from the tomb. If he did not Lazarus would die and I would be responsible. I assured him that I had acted with the best of intentions, meaning only to help spread his message to a wider audience. I bowed my head in shame, but suddenly felt his hand on my shoulder. Looking up, I saw the anger had left his face, and his eyes were gentle with compassion. We would go to Bethany, he said. He was impressed by the sacrifice Lazarus and his family had made for his sake, misguide though it was. But I must promise never again to make any similar decisions without consulting him first, no matter how much I might believe they would help him or the cause. I swore that I would obey him.

Then he asked me to promise to carry out any orders that he gave me in the future whether I agreed or approved of them or not. I must simply trust him and perform his commands without question. Again I gave my word, and he hugged me to him with a laugh, before leading me back into the courtyard, saying we had need of sleep before the journey.

None of the brothers was pleased when they woke to be informed by the Master that they were to set off for Bethany the following morning. There were still two party nights left! John complained the most bitterly, but the Master silenced him. Lazarus had fallen asleep, he said, and he must go to awaken him. I blushed at his words, so near were they to the truth, but you were all confused and there were more grumbles until the Master said that his decision was final. They would spend one more night of merriment and proceed to Bethany early the next day. He instructed me to go on ahead to warn Martha and Mary of his arrival, and kissing his hands gratefully I set off at once.

Jesus wept.
John 11:35

Travelling by night is not easy at the best of times, and on this occasion the moon was obscured by heavy cloud, so I tripped and stumbled many times over unseen stones. Although I tried to avoid stopping for the occasional rest, extreme fatigue made it necessary, so it was not until the sun was high next day when I reached Bethany.

The courtyard of Lazarus's home was filled with menfolk from the village, muttering prayers and lamentations. My eldest cousin came forward and embraced me mournfully before ushering me into the house.

The main room was packed with black-clothed women, seated on the floor, moaning and wailing, rocking their bodies and crooning dirges. They were grouped around Martha and Mary who crouched in a tight embrace; the headscarves pulled over their faces covered with the gray ash of mourning.

A passage was made for me and I knelt beside them to offer my condolence with a lump in my throat, so affected was I by the atmosphere of grief. Martha raised her kerchief when she heard my voice, and her glistening eyes questioned mine. I told her the Master was on his way. She heaved a deep sigh of relief.

"What have we done?" she whispered. "Look how much they loved him!"

"Just wait and see," I replied, "How much they will love the one who restores him to life!"

She looked at me strangely for a moment before lowering her veil and wrapping her sister even more closely in her arms. Slightly shaken, I backed out of the room and made my way up to the roof, where I resolved to wait and keep watch on the distant hill which the Master would descend on his arrival.

Below was a scene of deceptive tranquillity, with sparrows chirping in the olive-trees, and yellow butterflies floating past. I could see the tomb at the end of the garden, covered now by the circular stone behind which Lazarus slept. This was the second day of mourning. For everything to work perfectly the Master should arrive on the following day, preferably some time after noon, when Lazarus would have woken from his drugged sleep. And then what wonders would be performed!

The rhythmic chants of the men in the courtyard and the muffled keening of the women, together with the heat of the sun and my prolonged lack of sleep all contributed to a heavy drowsiness and I found it impossible to keep my eyes open. Lying down in the shade of the wall, I fell into a deep sleep.

When I awoke several hours later the sky was a black velvet dome sprinkled with stars. Hunger gnawed my belly like a rat, but I dared not go down to look for food. The house was in mourning, and fasting was the rule, I comforted myself with the thought that the next day the fast would become feast with the resurrection of Lazarus. I curled up again to dream, feeling proud that it was I who would have brought it about.

Martha brought me a cup of goat's milk in the morning, and I gulped it down thirstily. She told me that everything had gone according to plan, but she had not realized the effect it would have on her. The real tears, of those she knew and loved, for the faked death of her brother had moved her deeply. She knew that he would in fact die one day in the future, but she felt she had already lived that day.

I congratulated her and Mary on their performance, and assured her that the sacrifice they had made would not be forgotten when the Master established his Kingdom. She looked at me with tear-swollen eyes and asked what would happen if the Master did not arrive? If something should delay him—an accident perhaps? Lazarus would be trapped in the tomb and die of hunger or suffocation unless we released him ourselves, revealing the deception we had created. Patting her arm reassuringly, I told her to banish such fears from her mind. The Master would be on time. We must trust him.

But after she had left, the fears she had expressed remained and became mine. Imagine if what she dreaded should come true? How could we bring Lazarus back to life without exposing ourselves as frauds, hoaxers? And what explanation could we give once we had? The idea was a nightmare, and I thrust it from my brain. The Master would come. He must!

Shortly after midday Mary came with a cup of wine and bitter herbs. I took it and thanked her without moving my eyes from the distant crest of the hill. She told me that a wealthy customer named Joseph of Arimathea had come down from Jerusalem to offer his sympathy when he heard the news. He was an important man, a member of the Sanhedrin, and had known Lazarus personally as an acquaintance and fair dealer.

I asked Mary if she were afraid that the Master might not arrive in time, like Martha, but she shook her head confidently, saying that he would be there soon, and I must not lose faith. Taking my empty cup, she smiled encouragingly and went back downstairs.

And sure enough, just a short while later a little group of figures appeared on the hilltop and began making their way down, raising a cloud of dust as they came. My heart leapt with joy at the sight, and then all of a sudden froze with fear. Before, I had been anxious that the Master might arrive too late. Now I was afraid that he might have arrived too early! What a horrible predicament it would be if Lazarus had not woken and did not return to life when the Master ordered him to!

The sun was going down, staining the sky a bloody orange. Perhaps the time was right, but to make absolutely sure, I felt that the Master's arrival should be delayed a little longer.

I ran downstairs and found Martha still crouched in the midst of the mourners. I whispered the news of the Master's approach and my own fears as to the timing. She got up instantly and left the house without a word. I followed as she ran, her black mourning-garb fluttering in the fading gray of the twilight. The Master and men were soon in sight, coming towards us. He stopped as Martha approached, and she flung herself on the ground before him. As I drew nearer I heard her begging him to wait a while and calling him Christ, the Son of God who had been sent to save the world. Then, bidding us stay until her return, she hurried off back to Bethany.

I greeted the Master with a kiss, reading no trace of conspiracy in his calm demeanor. I heard grumbles and complaints from several of the disciples against Martha, wondering why she had made them wait there hungry, tired and thirsty when her house was so near. I was grateful to hear you admonish them for their whining, Peter.

We sat on the ground and waited for Martha's return. I noticed that the Master was accompanied by his mother. She was lovingly tidying his hair with a comb, her face bathed in tenderness, but the secret sorrow was still discernible. Suddenly, she stopped and met my gaze with a cold stare that made me look away. Had the Master confided in her about the miracle he was about to perform for me?

Then, in the darkness that had now fallen, we saw the light of flaming torches dancing towards us from Bethany. As they came closer the Master stood up, and we all rose with him. Soon a crowd of mourners had reached us, and the one who led them, Mary, fell weeping at the Master's feet.

May I remind you of the events that followed, Peter? I feel I must record them here as it all comes back to me. Martha and Mary weeping and complaining that Lazarus would not have died if the Master had been there. The shock I felt to see tears flowing from the Master's eyes. The curious murmurs of the crowd as they followed us back to the house and through the garden to the tomb. Martha's protestations when the Master ordered the stone to be rolled aside, saying that the body would have begun to decay. The grating sound as the stone was pushed away, and the black gaping hole which was revealed, the light from the torches flickering on the cliff walls around it. The command the Master gave for Lazarus to come forth, and the breathless hush that fell upon us all. And then the wave of panic that ran through the crowd as Lazarus slowly emerged from the tomb like a ghost, still wrapped in his shroud. The screaming and fainting of women, the shouts of glory and amazement as people fell to their knees to praise God. And the Master taking Lazarus in his arms and removing the cloth from his face, restoring him to his sisters, who kissed him frantically and took him promptly to his bed to rest after the ordeal he had been through, their faces streaming with tears of joy.

We returned to the house and courtyard, and a party to outrival the one we had left in Cana began, with music, song, wine and overflowing happiness to celebrate the resurrection of Lazarus.

During the celebrations I observed the Master deep in conversation with a wealthy-looking stranger. On inquiry I learned that it was the man from Jerusalem Mary had spoken of, Joseph of Arimathea. I gloated over the fact that we had gained such an influential follower.

News spread quickly through the village, and soon the courtyard was filled with others who had not been present, wanting to see the man who had raised Lazarus from the dead, and to touch him in the hope of benefiting from his magic power. The excitement became such that the Master was in danger of being mobbed, so we escorted him to the roof for safety, allowing only a selected few to join us, while the boisterous rejoicing continued in the courtyard below.

Glancing around at my fellow disciples, I noticed the expressions of stunned bewilderment on your faces. None of you quite understood what had happened, only that the Master had done something extraordinary, completely unexpected, and you regarded him with a new and undisguised awe. Guarded by a ring of protective brothers, he continued his talk with Joseph, breaking off occasionally to acknowledge the congratulations of admirers. How proud I felt that it was I who had initiated the miracle, and this wonderful celebration of the Master's power was all thanks to me. I was sure that he must be pleased with me for what I had done, even though he had ordered me never to act behind his back again.

Martha appeared at my side and asked me to come to Lazarus's room, so I slipped away with her. Lazarus was sitting up in bed, being fed soup from a bowl by Mary. The chatter and laughter that filtered into his room from downstairs was faint and muted. His body felt unnaturally light in my grasp as I embraced him. His pupils were dilated, and his cheekbones stood out in a way I had never noticed before. He began to laugh happily and triumphantly, and we joined him until his laughter died out in a long, rasping cough.

Our plan had worked, he gasped. We would gain uncountable converts to the Master's cause. He was proud for what he had done, but the experience had been terrible. He had woken in the tomb long before the arrival of the Master. It had been pitch black and silent and he felt icy cold. At first he hadn't known where he was, and then gradually it had all come back to him. He tried to relax and sleep, but it had been impossible, and soon he found it difficult to breathe, as the air in the small tomb was slowly used up. He became obsessed with a terror that the Master would not come, and fought against it with prayers and incantations. Eventually, just when he felt he could stand the cold and silence and darkness no more, the stone had slowly grated aside and light and air were his again. It had been a true miracle for him. And when he had heard the Master's voice calling him to come forth, he had risen and gone to him with a relief beyond description. How wonderful life was! How tragic that none of us really appreciated the miraculous wonder of being alive! Did we have to die to learn it?

He began to weep with little sobs, his face puckered like a baby. We hugged and kissed him, declaring our love and admiration. His tears turned to laughter, but it was high and hysterical, and soon interrupted by a spasm of hacking coughs. The sisters exchanged glances of concern, and Martha, caressing his brow, bade him be quiet and rest. He lay his head back on the pillow and closed his eyes, breathing with deep sighs.

I returned to the roof and found it carpeted with sleeping figures which was not surprising taking in account how far they had travelled that day and the excitement of the unexpected event that had resulted from their arrival. I, too, suddenly felt unbearably weary and, finding myself a space, lay down and sank into oblivion.

We were awakened early next morning with the news that a band of Temple police were on their way from Jerusalem with orders to arrest the Master and bring him in for questioning. A breathless servant of Joseph of Arimathea brought the tidings. Returning overnight to Jerusalem, he had discovered that the raising of Lazarus had already reached the ears of the Sanhedrin, who were outraged by its implications, fearing that rumors and excitement might cause the people to act foolishly and invoke the wrath of the Roman overlords. They were determined to put an end to the Master and his teaching, which they had learned of from their spies throughout the provinces. Joseph had sent us warning because, after having met the Master and witnessed his miracle, he had become convinced that he was the Expected One.

Having few possessions to gather, we were able to take flight immediately. The Master kissed his mother and bade her stay, asking Martha and Mary to look after her until his return, which they willingly promised to do.

Lazarus, still abed, looked very weak, but his coughing had ceased. Embracing him, I whispered my heartfelt thanks for all he had done. He smiled at me strangely. Since his experience of death, he said, he now knew the true value of life, and he intended to live it to the full. I would find him a changed man when next we met. I had no time to question his meaning, for the Master called, and with little more ado we were on our way to the hills of Samaria and safety.

Several weeks passed, and after a sojourn in Ephraim we crossed the waters of the Jordan to Perea where the Master preached some of his most inspired and inspiring sermons. And it was then that he announced we would spend the approaching Passover in Jerusalem.

Jerusalem! Our greatest challenge! The trial and testing place of all prophets! The culmination of the mission!

Along with the excitement caused by the decision, there were some questions to be asked. Was the Master ready for the ultimate exposure in the city of cities? Were we capable of spreading the word successfully in such a crowded, cosmopolitan place, especially during the Holy Feast? Would it be the final glorification and acceptance of him as the Messiah, or could it end in abject disappointment and the liquidation of all we had fought for? We talked long into the night, each airing a different opinion, which was disputed and pondered upon.

None of us knew exactly what to expect, but it was with hearts filled with hope that we took the road back to Bethany, there to spend Passover eve before the entrance of the Master into Jerusalem the following day.

Now, Peter, if you have borne with me thus far, you will have learned the answers to some questions which may have puzzled you, and read much that you know already. Forgive my rambling. I have tried to contain myself, but the memories flood back and my hand often seems to move across the page despite myself. You may condemn me for some of the things that I did, but I hope you will understand that they were only done for the glorification of the Master.

However, what I am about to relate to you now—the orders I was given, and what I did to prevent the disastrous results that would have occurred if I had carried them out—I'm sure you will understand and forgive. If I had done as he ordered, you would not now be back in Jerusalem proclaiming the resurrection and rousing souls with his message of love! All hopes, all expectations, all the glory of the harvest would have perished with him on the cross. Please read on. Understand my motives. And forgive me.

*Then entered Satan into Judas surnamed Iscariot,
being of the number of the twelve.*
Luke 22:3

Warmly welcomed by the villagers of Bethany after three months absence, we warned them to keep our presence a secret and they promised to do so. Martha and Mary rejoiced to see us again, and the Master and his mother embraced lovingly.

A message was sent to Lazarus in Jerusalem. After the news of his resurrection had spread he had become a celebrity, and many people had come down to Bethany to see him. One of the visitors, the widow of a rich spice merchant, had proposed marriage shortly after their first meeting, and Lazarus had accepted without hesitation and gone to live with her in the city. His sisters assured me that his wife was a good woman, who was a devoted disciple of the Master's teaching, but still I was shocked, and when he arrived alone that evening to greet us, I voiced my disquiet on his hasty nuptials, but he merely laughed and said he had told me that he intended to seize his chances in life, and if a rich widow was one of them, why then, she was to be seized! He appeared healthy and happy, and I could not be angry with him, but was disturbed by his flippant tone and sudden mercenary attitude.

We ate and drank well that night; up on the roof under the stars, sharing a sense of elation, as if our goal was in sight and the morrow would be our making. Talk flowed along with the wine, and plans were laid out. The Master gave his orders in a strangely detached manner, as though there were something on his mind that he had not yet clarified. I remember your indignation, Peter, when he instructed Philip to fetch a she-ass to be his mount in the morning, saying that it would be more fitting for him to be astride a fiery stallion for his entrance into the city. We agreed, but the Master silenced us with a quotation from Zechariah:

"Rejoice greatly, O daughter of Zion; shout, O daughter of Jerusalem: behold, thy King cometh unto thee: he is just, and having salvation; lowly, and riding upon an ass, and upon a colt the foal of an ass."

He reminded us that the horse was a symbol of war, and he had come to bring peace. The scriptures must be fulfilled, he said—a phrase which had begun to crop up in his speech more and more frequently.

I managed to change the disgruntled mutterings to laughter by asking which he intended to ride upon, the ass or the foal? Or, if the scriptures were to be fulfilled, would he have to ride on both at the same time? The Master, too, smiled at my joke, then, as he began to instruct us on the way we should behave in the city, Mary appeared at my side and whispered that a visitor had arrived who I should see.

Rising reluctantly, I followed her downstairs, reminding her that such interruptions had been specifically forbidden. She apologized, but the stranger had been adamant and mentioned my name as well as the Master's, and she had thought it more appropriate that I should deal with him.

The man waiting outside turned round at the sound of our footsteps. He was no stranger to me. It was Blind Bartimeus from Jericho!

Dismissing Mary, I ushered him into the courtyard and asked what he wanted. He was dressed in the same rags that I had last seen him in, but the blank stare worn in his "blindness" had been replaced by a bitter, shifty expression. Looking at me disdainfully, he replied that it was the Master he wished to speak to. I told him that he was busy and could not be disturbed, but I would gladly pass on any message he wished to convey. He laughed cynically and asked if I would be so kind as to ask him if he would perform another miracle and make him blind again? Sternly, I asked him what he meant, and he told me his story.

He had lost his livelihood. Before, when he was 'blind', he had at least been able to make enough to afford to fill his belly every day thanks to the charity of sympathetic passers-by. It may not have been an honest living, but he had managed to live. Then I had come along and ruined everything. After his "cure" he had been brought before the Pharisees and asked to explain the sudden restoration of his sight. They had been outraged by his reply that the Master was the Messiah and had performed a miracle through the will of God. He had been thrown out of the synagogue and threatened with punishment for blasphemy. And when he had returned to his begging place at the gate, nobody would give him any money. They told him to get a job and stop sponging off others. That was all very well for them to say, but what work was he capable of? He was too old and lazy to learn a trade, and when he looked around at the options open to the unskilled laborer, the choices were not tempting. They were dirty, tiring and degrading. How much more appealing was his old way of life! Simply sitting in the shade against the wall, gossiping with his fellow beggars and relying on the kindness of passing strangers.

The money I had given him soon petered away, and he was reduced to a state of penury he had never experienced in his life. He blamed me for it all. I must give him some more money. Otherwise, he said, he would be tempted to expose the miracle as a fake and the Master as a charlatan. I quietly pointed out that if he did such a thing it would also reveal the fact that he had not been blind in the first place, and had spent his life cheating and defrauding people. As a result he could expect the stigma of branding or even death by stoning.

He hadn't thought of that, and his jaw dropped at the prospect. I tried to appeal to his better nature by reminding him of the promised Kingdom, and the wonderful things it would bring, hut he silenced me. It was a fine idea, he said, but how long would we have to wait for it to happen? In the meantime he had an empty belly, and money was the only way to fill it.

Realizing that there was no arguing with him, I reached for

the purse at my belt, counted out a number of coins, and pressed them into his hand. Peering at them and fingering them greedily, he said he had to have more. He couldn't last for a week on such a pittance. Exasperated, I explained that we were going up to Jerusalem for the Passover Feast the next day and it was all I could part with. I told him it could be the culmination of our mission, and that the Kingdom might be nearer than he thought. He snorted in derision and said that it had better come soon or he would be forced to have a relapse and become blind again, which wouldn't look very good for the Master. Miracles were meant to last!

I escorted him out into the street, warning him that there was no point in seeking us out again, for he would get no more money, no matter what he threatened. With an obscene gesture of farewell he shuffled away in the dark and with a disgusted relief I returned to the roof.

I found you had all bedded down for the night, except for the Master, who was seated on the low parapet wall, gazing at the stars. He got up as I emerged from the stairwell and asked where I had been. I told him the story of Bartimaeus and his plight. The Master laughed softly and pointed out that this was the result of acting without consulting him on the matter. I had reaped what I had sown.

Then, putting his arm around my shoulder, he said that he would like to walk for a while in the garden before retiring, and would be pleased if I would accompany him. I was surprised at this sudden honor, for the Master seldom gave any of us, apart from John, the privilege of his company alone. Glowing with pride, I descended the stairs with him, relishing the closeness of his body.

We wandered for a time among the trees, listening to the chirrup of the crickets and watching the erratic dance of the fireflies. The moon was bright, and I glanced occasionally at the Master's face, bathed in its silvery light. I was filled with a blissful contentment.

After a while he dropped his arm and, leaning back against the gnarled branch of an olive-tree, gazed up at the sky. Then he spoke.

In a quiet voice he asked if I remembered the promise I had made to do anything he asked, whether I agreed with it or not. I said that I did, and would keep my word. He paused for a while before he continued. Then he said that when we got to Jerusalem he wanted me to go to the Temple priests and betray him.

At first I thought I had misheard his words, and asked him to repeat what he had said. Calmly and slowly he did so. I was stunned. Had he gone mad? I didn't understand. Why should I do such a thing? The Temple priests considered his growing reputation a threat to their authority. He would be arrested and charged with some fabricated crime. They might even have him executed! What he was suggesting was dangerous nonsense. After all our work, all his preaching, and the number of followers he had gained, why should he decide to put himself in the hands of the enemy and plunge the movement into dismal failure? I was utterly bewildered.

Putting a hand on my shoulder, hr told me to trust him. He had thought the whole thing out and come to the conclusion that it was the best way to ensure our triumph. The Sanhedrin were itching to get hold of him, it was true, but they would not dare to have him arrested in the crowded streets of Jerusalem during the feast, surrounded as he would be by followers and admirers, for fear of sparking off a riot that they would find difficult to explain to their Roman overlords. But they would jump at the chance to seize him unguarded in some quiet place. Once they had him in their clutches, what charges could they find to bring against him? He was not a criminal. All he preached was love and brotherhood.

I tried to continue my protestations but he silenced me, saying that I need not worry for his safety. There was a major factor that would protect him from their machinations. We were going up to Jerusalem to celebrate the feast of the Passover, and did I not remember that Roman jurisdiction had decreed that a prisoner of popular choice must be released to the Jewish people on that day? Who would that prisoner be but himself? His followers would demand his reprieve, and they could not he refused by law. He would be freed by the will of his flock, the news of his release would spread throughout the city, and countless more would hear of him and join the movement. Could I not see the logic in his plan?

I could. A vision of the Master carried shoulder-high away from his impotent captors by a jubilant crowd chanting triumphant hallelujahs flashed before my eyes. But at the same time I was terribly afraid. What if they abused or humiliated him while in their custody? I could not bear the thought and asked him again to reconsider, but he replied that his mind was resolved. I must go the next day to the high priests of the Temple and offer to hand him over to them for a ransom, and make sure that I got a good price! He warned me to tell no one of our plan. Total secrecy was in order if we were to succeed.

I voiced another anxious thought. The others would believe that I was a real traitor, They would shun and despise me. With a quiet chuckle he admitted they might, but it would not be for long. After his release he would inform them that I had been acting on orders and I would be considered a hero for my courage. A traitorous disciple was essential for the authentic touch, he said, and I had shown such cunning initiative in my previous endeavors that he had chosen me. I flushed with embarrassment and could say nothing. Telling me to be brave and not fail him, he kissed me on the cheek and walked slowly back to the house.

I lingered for a while in the garden, my thoughts filled with confusion. It was an audacious plan, a brilliant strategy, but it had come as a shock to me that the Master, too, could resort to such methods to further his cause. And still the thought that it might not work out as simply as he predicted worried me terribly. You can understand my dilemma, Peter. Would you have agreed to carry out such an order without a qualm?

After long, tortured speculation I returned to the roof, lay down among the sleepers, and tried to abandon myself to slumber but it was impossible. Just as I was dropping off I would suddenly wake, remembering with horror what the Master had asked me to do. I dreaded the dawn.

*The disciple is not above his master: but everyone
that is perfect shall be as his master.*
Luke 6:40

But dawn it did, and after yawning, stretching and sleepy ablutions, the men were awake with an excitement that seemed to increase with the rising of the sun. None seemed to notice my mood of depression except the Master, who cast me the occasional knowing smile, which contributed little to my confidence. I felt isolated and remote, already an outcast for the deed I was to perform.

After breakfast, Philip was sent to collect for the ass, and Martha and Mary brought some of the best wine to give us spirit. James and John caused some ill-feeling among the group by asking for privileged places on either side of the Master when he sat in judgement of sinners after the Kingdom was established, but we were delighted at the way he shamed them into silence by declaring that those who exalted themselves would be lowered and those who humbled themselves would be exalted.

Mary came to my side and whispered that a stranger had arrived asking to see the Master. I went downstairs with her, angry that she had admitted yet another visitor. We were supposed to be there in secrecy, and yet she was allowing open house to all callers. She said that he was not like the other man. There was something special about him. He looked like a wretched beggar, but his voice and manner were educated. The expression of sorrow and despair on his face when she had told him that he could not see the Master had touched her heart, so she had told him to wait, and decided to call me to interrogate him.

The stranger in the courtyard did resemble a poor mendicant. He was dressed in a torn, filthy robe, tied at the waist with a piece of rope. His hair and beard were long and unkempt, but the eyes that stared beseechingly from his dirty sunburned face reminded me very much of the Master's. I asked him what he wanted.

"I have done it," he said. The voice, soft and cultured, contradicted his appearance.

I didn't understand. I asked what it was that he had done.

"I have done as the Master bade me. Sold all my possessions, given the money to the poor, and come to follow him. I've been searching for him for so long. Do you not remember me?"

And then suddenly, to my astonishment, I did. But his appearance was so altered from the last time we had met that he seemed an entirely different person.

It was the rich young man who had come to see the Master while he was preaching in Decapolis. The son of a wealthy governor, he had approached the Master after one of his sermons, asking him how he could gain eternal life. He had been clad then in costly and beautiful clothes, decorated with gold and jewels, his hair oiled and styled, his body fragrant with perfume. He had spoken humbly and reverently, but when he addressed him as "Good Master", the Master had retorted that nothing was "good" but God. If he wished to gain a place in Heaven he should follow the Commandments strictly. The young man said that he had obeyed them all his life. At this the Master had smiled warmly and announced that if it were so, there was but one thing lacking. He should renounce his wealth, sell all that he had, give the money to the poor and then come and follow him. There was a silence, and the young man had lowered his eyes and sadly walked away.

The Master had told us to observe how difficult it was for a rich man to enter Heaven. It was easier, he said, for a camel to pass through the eye of a needle than for a rich man to get into the Kingdom of God.

But there he stood before me, our rich young man, stripped of all his finery, clothed in rags, abased and humbled. He had returned home after his conference with the Master, he said, and spent several days in troubled contemplation before coming to his decision. Then, casting all doubts aside, he had put the Master's advice into action, paying generous last wages to his servants, freeing his slaves and selling off his property to the usurers who came swarming like flies when they heard of the bargain prices, until everything he had was gone, the money distributed among the astonished poor of his province.

His father, astonished at the news of his son's behavior, had come to reason with him, but seeing him so determined, had given up in rage, disowning him and cursing him for a fool. But the young man had felt no regret or remorse. He felt spiritually reborn; his worldly cares disposed of along with his wealth. His only concern was to find the Master and join him, and that he had set out to do, even exchanging the last rich garments on his back with those of a poor beggar he met on the road. He had inquired along the way for news of the Master and been directed to different locations, only to be told when he arrived that he had missed him by days or hours, and so his quest had stretched on endlessly, but the burning hope of finding him had kept him resolute, no matter how hungry and exhausted he had become. And was his search over? Had he found him at last?

Without a word I took his arm and led him upstairs to the roof. I could find nothing to say, so awed was I by the incredible sacrifice he had made for the sake of the Master. There was no question of turning him away; his perseverance had to be rewarded. I guided him out into the sunlight and the presence of the Master, who stood with cup in hand, seemingly concluding an amusing anecdote, for you all laughed loud and long until aware of an alien presence, at which you broke off and stared suspiciously at the stranger with me.

He broke away from me and ran and knelt before the Master, grasping his hand and kissing it feverishly. The Master stooped, and raising him to his feet, gently rebuked him, saying no man should kneel before another. Then he glanced questioningly at me. I said he was a visitor that I could not find it in my heart to turn away. Let him listen to his story and he would know why.

And so the young man related the same tale to the Master. We learned his name. It was Darius.

When he had finished there were tears in the Master's eyes. He opened his arms wide and embraced Darius, kissing him lovingly on both cheeks. Then, turning to the rest of us, he announced that we were witnessing a true miracle. A camel had passed through the eye of a needle! Here was a rich man become a true believer, ready to sell all to buy the pearl of great price, one who had sacrificed more than any of us to gain eternal life.

Forgive me, Peter Again I am relating events at which you were present. But owing to the great debt that we all owe Darius, I cannot avoid recording his meeting with the Master and the effect it had upon us all.

Darius staggered, and seemed on the point of collapse. The Master helped him to sit and inquired how long it had been since he last broke fast. Darius said that a passing traveler had given him some bread a couple of days before. The Master told Martha to bring food immediately, and he held his own cup to Darius's lips, helping him to drink. I could not help but smile at John's peevish look of jealousy.

After he had eaten some bread and grapes, Lazarus and the Master took Darius downstairs, and when they returned, he was transformed. The dirt had been washed from his face, his hair and beard trimmed, oiled and combed, and he was dressed in one of Lazarus's clean white robes. Again I was struck by his resemblance to the Master, in their features, bearing, and the unfathomable expression of peace in their eyes. They might even have been taken for brothers.

When we sat down, the Master placed Darius on his right, at which John could contain himself no longer, complaining that he had always sat there. The Master told him not to be jealous, and said that Darius had humbled himself, and therefore deserved to be exalted. John folded his arms and sat seething, his mouth a grim line.

Martha and the Master's mother brought bowls of pottage as a final meal before our departure, and we ate in silence, each with his own private thoughts. The Master fed Darius lovingly with his own hand.

Suddenly Mary appeared and slowly approached the Master, carrying a small flask of nard. Standing behind him, she broke it open and poured it over his head. We were all stunned by her unexpected action. John pushed her roughly away with an oath. The sweet scent of the perfume reached my nostrils, and I angrily admonished her for such waste, for it was obviously expensive. We would have done better to have sold it and given the money to the poor. You all voiced your agreement, indignant at her extravagance, but the Master said she had done a beautiful thing. The poor would always be there for us to help, but he would not. She was merely anointing him in preparation for his burial. And was not the expected Messiah also to be known as the Anointed One? Yes, muttered Thomas, but not by a whore, And you, Peter, complained that she had made the Master smell like one.

I could not join in the laughter. My blood had frozen at his words of anointing and burial, reminding me of the task that awaited me in Jerusalem. Who could predict what would happen once I had turned his willing body over to the wily priests of the Sanhedrin?

At that moment Philip appeared and announced that the donkeys were waiting downstairs. The Master invited him to rest and drink after his tiresome mission, but he had already drunk with the donkeys' owner and was keen to be on the way to Jerusalem, as time was passing.

And so the Master rose, and all of us with him. After blessing Martha and Mary, he bade them take care of his mother until his return. She, clinging to him, begged him not to go, for she had had a dream of ill-foreboding, but he gently removed her hold and kissed her on the forehead, promising that he would return soon. Wishing the women a happy Passover, he descended the steps to the street, and we all followed.

A crowd of waiting villagers cheered and clapped when the Master appeared, some of them waving palm leaves. The Master told us to gather palms branches along the route and do likewise, and ordered a couple of brothers to go ahead to the gates of Jerusalem to advertise his arrival. If any of us got separated from the group in the city, a possibility due to the multitudes that would be there, we were to find our way to the house of Joseph of Arimathea, where we were to celebrate our Passover supper. Then he reminded us that we were to act strictly according to the personal instructions he had given each of us. He looked meaningfully at me when he said this, and my heart sank. He was still determined that I should betray him.

The condition of the two donkeys was poor and I remember you, Peter, asking if better could not have been found? You said they were unworthy of the Master and would make him an object of ridicule, but he merely smiled and stroked the muzzle of the she-ass, saying that they would suffice. Then, he announced that Darius was still exhausted from his long search, and it would unduly tire him to walk the two or more miles to Jerusalem, so he would ride beside him on the colt. John let out an involuntary yelp of outrage, but suppressed himself after a stern look from the Master. Darius protested that he was not worthy of such an honor, but the Master said he was worthy of greater, and perhaps it would be even more suitable for him to ride the she-ass, at which suggestion Darius mounted the young colt without demur. An enthusiastic villager spread his cloak over the back of its mother, the Master took his seat, and with a wave of his hand we were off.

A small crowd from Bethany accompanied us, singing and chanting and throwing their cloaks under the hooves of the Master's beast to cushion its step and, no doubt, to brag in later years that they owned a cloak over which the Master had ridden on his triumphant procession to Jerusalem.

The young foal, alarmed by the noise, kept close to its mother, so Darius and the Master rode abreast. Darius's feet almost touched the ground and the Master was jolted up and down; but for the calm and resolute expressions upon their faces, they would have presented a sight for ridicule.

As we rounded the crest of a hill, Jerusalem suddenly came into view. The Master halted his donkey; we all ceased chanting and stared in silence at the city. I had seen it often enough in the past, but was impressed by the sight as always. From its strategic position thick protective walls rose majestically, surrounding towers, roofs and turrets, and the magnificent golden dome of the Temple glittering in the sun. We could see tiny figures streaming in and out through the gates. The faint hum of the distant calls, chants and chatter created the impression of a gigantic beehive. Many of our brothers from Galilee, you included, Peter, had never seen Jerusalem before, and your mouths hung open as you gazed in awe at the holy city.

Turning to the Master, we were astonished to see that he was weeping. He gazed ahead, tears rolling unchecked down his cheeks. In a choking voice he cried that they would never accept him. This was Jerusalem, the city which murdered the prophets and stoned the messengers God sent to her. Its inhabitants were blind, and they and the city would all be destroyed because of their refusal to accept the true word of God.

We comforted him with reassuring words. He would be recognized. This was the city where he would be enthroned, from which he would rule in righteousness and justice. Others may have suffered there in the past, but God would protect him. He was the Chosen One. He need fear no harm.

Wiping his eyes silently with his sleeve, the Master spurred the ass onward with his heels. I stood and watched for a moment as the little band of dusty followers resumed chanting and palm-branch waving around the two men on their bony, stumbling donkeys. They suddenly seemed a heartbreakingly pathetic sight, and the Master's talk of murdered prophets and stoned messengers had sent a shiver of foreboding down my spine.

> *Then one of the twelve, called Judas Iscariot, went unto the chief priests, And said unto them, What will ye give me, and I will deliver him unto you? And they covenanted with him for thirty pieces of silver And from that time he sought opportunity to betray him.*
> Matthew 26:14-16

Our entry into Jerusalem was not the triumphant occasion we had imagined it would be. The gateway was crowded with pilgrims and traders coming and going, but we managed to create a lane for the Master and Darius by marching on either side of them, waving our palm-leaves and shouting hosannas, forcing the people to step aside.

A small group of cheering followers had gathered to welcome the Master, but they were far outnumbered by the other folk going about their business, who seemed puzzled and irritated by the temporary obstruction we were causing. Many stopped to stare at our curious procession.

Others came forward to ask what was going on. I told them that the Messiah had come, the King of Righteousness who was to deliver our country. One man asked which one he was, and, glancing at the Master and Darius riding along side by aide, I could understand his confusion. A street trader arched his eyebrow cynically at my reply and exclaimed, "Nor another one!" When I asked what he meant, he said that he had already witnessed the arrival of three other Messiahs and their followers that day. He laughed and slapped me on the back, saying, "May the best man win!" and went back to hawking his wares.

As we emerged into the huge square before the Temple I noticed that our arrival seemed to be just another Passover distraction, and the choice was manifold. The square was bustling and noisy, filled with moneychangers, refreshment stalls, sheep, goats, cows, camels and birds to be purchased for sacrifice. Speakers stood here and there on upturned barrels: Zealots, Essenes, Pharisees, and general rabble-rousers haranguing their listeners with different messages.

We stopped, and the Master and Darius dismounted. With a conspiratorial wink, the Master told me to be about my business, and then, with an arm around Darius, he gestured to the rest of you and ventured forth into the thronging crowds of the square.

I was left alone, and looking up at the towering splendor of the Temple I could understand why the mouths of my brothers had hung open. There is probably not a more impressive building in the world, and I felt tiny and humble as I mounted the steps and made my way through the beautiful cloisters of marble to the upper level and the Temple proper.

But although the outside of the Temple is magnificent, the inside is quite a different matter. The mingled odor of freshly spilled blood, animal excrement and cloying incense, along with the echoing sacred chants of the Levites, half-drowned by the frantic screams of the sacrificial beasts in the darkling gloom, has always seemed to me like a scene from a nightmare. I had to hold my breath in order to stop myself from retching.

I found an idle Temple acolyte leaning against a pillar and told him that I wanted to speak to the High Priests. He looked down his nose and asked me my business. I said that it was highly important; I had information to convey in which they would be very interested, and he would probably be rewarded for it if he showed me to them. Disdainfully he detached himself from the pillar and led me down many a grand corridor until we reached a chamber hung with purple and crimson drapery. In it sat a group of High Priests, laughing boisterously together as they counted piles of **gold and silver coins which visiting pilgrims had exchanged for the sacred shekel of the Temple in order to purchase their sacrificial** animals. Their laughter ceased and they looked warily up as I was brought in by the suddenly obsequious underling, who gushed that he believed I had news to relate that might be to their advantage.

All eyes were turned to me, and there was an expectant silence. As I looked at their bloated bodies in their rich robes, the oiled and curled beards which hung from their over-fed faces, and the greedy, haughty look in their eyes, I felt a sudden surge of anger and wanted to shout out my vilification of them like the Baptist had done. They were parasites and hypocrites, their elaborate rituals and rigmarole simply meaningless trash with which they deluded our people for their own gain. But I could not. Apart from the fact that I would probably be instantly arrested, I had promised the Master to follow his instructions expressly, whether I understood them or not. So instead I stammered out that I was willing to betray a man in whom I believed they had some interest.

With an air of detached boredom, one of them asked for his name, while another slipped out a ledger, dipped a reed into ink, and wrote as I gave the Master's name. The others listened, and one or two said they had never heard of him. The inscriber smugly mentioned Galilee, and the ignorant ones gave little murmurs of recognition. Then he turned to me and asked what charges could be brought against him.

I had not been prepared for that, and I groped for words. He preached liberation, I said; revolution against Roman rule; universal love and brotherhood. The reed scratched across the parchment, and, after a pause, the priest looked up and asked if I considered such charges worthy of arrest? I hesitated. They seemed to want something more. I decided to stretch the truth a little, and answered that many people had called him the Messiah, and he had not denied the claim.

The reed flew across the page and ended with a with a flourish, a satisfied smile on the writer's face. He asked my name and place of abode. I said that I refused to give either until the reward was in my hands. At this, knowing looks passed between the priests, and they told me that so many informers had offered to betray trouble-makers in the past, only to disappear without fulfilling their obligations once they had been paid, that a new rule had been introduced. Money would not change hands until the victim was safely in theirs.

When I asked how much it would be, I was told that the reward would be thirty pieces of silver. I gasped in surprise. It was a pittance for a man as important as the Master was, and I told them so. They shrugged and said that I could take it or leave it. I shouldn't be so greedy. It was the standard fee for betrayals, and they weren't prepared to increase it for me or anyone else. Saying that I would have to consider the offer, I turned and left the chamber, escorted by the assistant who had brought me to them.

I felt dirty as I emerged from the gloom into the sunshine, as though I tainted by the very air I had shared with those smug, scheming hypocrites. I prayed that the Master would see sense and change his mind. Surely he would not allow himself to be handed over to them for a mere thirty pieces of silver?

For the first time I dreaded an encounter with the Master. I dawdled reluctantly on my way to the Upper City, where I had learned the house of Joseph of Arimathea was situated. It was late afternoon when I reached it, and as I entered the gates I was astonished to think that we were to be entertained in such a grand mansion. However, a servant who met me at the front door directed me to the courtyard at the back, where a room above a stable had been made available for our Passover supper.

Mounting the stairs, I found a workroom used for storing tools. A space had been cleared in the centre for a long, low table laid with platters and goblets ready for our meal.

Darius, standing at a small, grilled window gazing out over the city, was the only one there. He turned and greeted me with a smile. He told me the Master had given the others permission to go out and see the sights without him. I had missed a scene in the temple-square after I had left them. The Master had lost his temper and kicked over the tables of several money-changers and released doves from their cages, and many of the brothers had copied him until they had been chased away by an angry crowd. The Master was upstairs praying, but he had given orders for me to go to him as soon as I arrived. He pointed to a doorway at the back of the room. I went through it and climbed up a ladder, my legs trembling.

The sun was going down as I emerged on the flat roof, painting the sky in glorious shades of red and pink. In the distance the marble columns of the Temple glowed with a rosy light and the gold of its dome shone like fire. The Master knelt in the middle of the roof, his eyes closed. His face was calm and peaceful, and his lips moved silently as though he spoke to some unseen listener. I felt like an intruder, and was about to creep away, when he suddenly opened his eyes and saw me.

He stood and I went to him. After embracing me briefly in welcome, he laughingly asked how much I had got for him. I told him of my encounter with the priests and the amount that had been offered, payable only on delivery. The smile left his face and his eyes flashed angrily. It was an insult, he said—the standard price of a slave! Hope rose in my heart, and I said that of course he would not agree to be sold for so little. We would abandon his scheme. He looked at me darkly and said that we would certainly not. The money was not important. We would continue with the plan, and I would hand him over to them that very night!

I fell to my knees and implored him not to go through with it, telling him of the loathsome feeling I had had in their presence. They were vicious and cruel. I could not bear the thought of being the instrument for delivering him into their hands, but he was adamant, and raised me up firmly to my feet. He would not be long in their clutches, he said. Did he have to remind me of the Passover Amnesty granted the next day? He would be the one chosen to be released by popular demand, and once freed could not be arrested again. Could I not imagine how those hypocrites would squirm as the Kingdom of God was ushered in, knowing that by their own greed and cunning they had unwittingly helped to bring it about? I pleaded and protested, but he silenced me by reminding me of my promise to do all that he ordered without question. Then he outlined the plan for his arrest.

I was to share the Passover supper that evening with the rest of the brothers so that there would be no questions about my absence. During the meal the Master would give me a signal when to leave and return to the Temple. After he had dipped a piece of bread in the sauce bowl and handed it to me, I must get up immediately and go. That night he and the men would be sleeping in the Garden of Gethsemane, just outside the city walls. He would remove himself a little distance from the others in the company of Peter, James and John. He would also have Darius with him, he added as an afterthought. I would lead the Temple police to the garden and find him there. In order that there should be no confusion as to who was to be arrested, I should inform them that the Master was the one I would approach and kiss in greeting. Then he would be seized, and what happened thereafter lay in the hands of God.

It was a simple and straightforward plan, yet it was what may happen thereafter that terrified me. I began to stammer out my doubts and fears, but he silenced me again, telling me to leave him, as he wished to be alone to pray. He kissed me on both cheeks, an example of how I should identify him that night in the garden. Then he knelt down and closed his eyes, and realizing that I could do nothing to dissuade him, I left the roof and descended the ladder, feeling the most miserable creature in existence.

The others had still not arrived, and Darius, like the Master, was kneeling quietly in prayer when I entered the room. My face obviously betrayed my thoughts, for on seeing me, he got up and came to me, asking what was wrong. He put an arm around my shoulder, and, unable to control myself, I burst into tears. He led me to a low platform and sat me down, murmuring soothing words and patting me gently on the back. Gradually I managed to calm myself, and again he asked me the cause of my distress. When I replied that the Master had forbidden me to tell anyone, he begged me to confide in him, saying that he would keep what I told him a secret, and that a problem shared was half resolved. His voice was so kind and concerned that I could not stop myself. I poured out to Darius the whole story of the Master's plan and the orders I had reluctantly agreed to perform.

He sat in silence when I had finished, staring into space, his brow creased in thought. Then he spoke. I must not do it, be said. If I delivered him into their hands it would be the end of the mission. Once they had him they would find a way of getting rid of him, even if the whole of Jerusalem clamored for his release. He was a thorn in their side that they wished to extract at all costs. It was suicide for the Master to submit to them. I agreed with him, but what could I do? He had ordered it.

Darius rose, saying that he would go and try to persuade him to change his mind, but I clung to his sleeve and begged him not to. I had already put forward all arguments against his scheme, but he was determined, and he would be furious with me for confiding in another against his strict instructions.

Darius sat down again and was silent for a while. Then he said that he could see only one other alternative. Eagerly, I asked him what it was. He replied that it should not be the Master who I handed over, but a substitute. Himself.

Before I could speak, he quickly outlined his plan. When I led the police to them in the garden, it must not be the Master that I kissed, but Darius, who would then be seized and taken away, leaving the Master free.

I was so stunned that I could not speak for a few seconds. Hope welled up in my heart like the waters of a hot spring. There was the chance that it could work. The priests only knew the Master by description, and Darius was very similar in appearance. But was he willing to suffer the humiliation and torture they might be inflicted upon him?

Darius said he was. The Master meant everything to him. For him he had given up wealth and title, and been disowned by his family. Every blow struck against him would be one the Master had been spared from, and his own death in his place would leave the Master alive and free to continue spreading the message of the Kingdom. And had the Master himself not said that no love was greater than to lay down one's life for one's friend?

Suddenly warned of the arrival of the brothers, by a chorus of discordant psalms outside, I quickly told Darius that I would do as he suggested and kiss him in the garden instead of the Master. But I warned him that while under arrest he must remain absolutely silent and not utter a word to betray himself or the Master, no matter how provoked. That way no positive charges could be brought against him. And if he behaved gently and meekly he might win the respect of his captors. Neither was his release unfeasible at the granting of the Passover Amnesty, if the crowd believed him to be the Master. Darius replied that he would put his trust in God. I embraced him lovingly and gratefully, as you, my brothers, staggered up the steps and into the room, filling it with song.

That last supper we all shared together remains etched upon my mind. I remember Joseph entering with servants bearing food and wine, apologizing sheepishly for not being able to entertain us in his own house. He had other guests to whom he was obliged, and he hoped we understood that in his position to be seen in the Master's company might make things difficult for him. The Master laughed and forgave him, saying that the day was coming when we would all be able to sit down together in God's Kingdom without fear or shame. Joseph kissed his hand and left, wishing us a happy Passover.

I remember the embarrassment we felt when the Master insisted on washing our feet. We could not understand his meaning, and it was hateful to see him abase himself before us. He told us that it was a lesson in humility. If he, our Master, could do such a thing for us, we should be prepared to do the same thing for each other. Neither did we understand when he called the bread his body and the wine his blood, and, passing it around, bade us eat and drink him.

And none of you understood when the Master announced that one of us was going to betray him. I flushed hotly at his words, not having expected them and flashed a conspiratorial glance at Darius, who returned it, while the rest of the brothers stared at each other stupefied, murmuring in disbelief. Darius was sitting in the honored place at the right of the Master, and you, Peter, turned to him and told him to inquire which of us he meant. Darius leaned forward and whispered the question.

The Master answered that it was the one he would give a piece of bread to after he had dipped it in the dish. Then he tore off a crust from a loaf, soaked it in the sauce and handed it deliberately across the table to me. The room fell silent. I took the sop with a trembling hand and sat there staring at it, not daring to look up.

The Master's voice, sharp and commanding roused me from my trance, telling me to be quick about my business. I stumbled up blindly from the table, and without a word went quickly out into the night, the damp bread clenched in my fist.

I
*Then Judas, which had betrayed him, when he saw
that he was condemned, repented himself, and
brought again the thirty pieces of silver to the chief
priests and elders,
Saying, I have sinned in that I have betrayed the
innocent blood. And they said, What is that to us?
see thou to That*
Matthew 27:3-4

As I made my way down through the dark streets towards the Temple, a fierce indignation burned in my heart. The Master had exposed me in front of all my brothers! He had not mentioned that as part of his plan. I had presumed that all would have been performed covertly, but instead he had talked openly of betrayal and explicitly branded me as the traitor with his overly dramatic gesture of handing me the piece of bread.

I put it into my mouth and clenched it between my teeth as I walked quickly on, trying to suppress my feelings of outrage. A hellish business lay before me, and I thanked God that he had sent Darius as a willing scapegoat to save the unsuspecting Master's life. I shuddered to imagine what my feelings would have been had he not volunteered himself, and had I really been on my way to betray the Master.

It was late when I arrived at the Temple, but there were still some sacrifices going on, and I found the attendant who had helped me before, yawning and leaning against the same pillar. I told him I had made up my mind, and was ready to betray the Master.

He nodded without a word, and I followed him down the same corridors, now illuminated by flaming torches, to the room I had been interviewed in before. I recognized some of the High Priests, but others were new to me. This time they were not as condescending when I stated my mission. News of the Master's behavior among the moneychangers in the market place had reached their ears, and they were more eager than ever to put a stop to him. The Chief High Priest, Caiaphas, had been particularly incensed. He wished to interview the Master personally, and it was to his house he was to be conveyed after the arrest.

After I had told them where the Master was to be found and my method of identifying him, I was led to a courtyard where Temple police were lolling and drinking. There were reluctant groans when they were told that an arrest was to be made. It was late, they complained and asked for it to be postponed until the next day, but they were silenced by the angry bark of a High Priest, and stood sullenly to attention. They were an ugly bunch of thugs, and several of them were drunk. The High Priest shouted more orders, and after fetching their swords and staves and taking burning torches and lanterns from the walls, they fell into rank. Then, after the priest had explained their mission, they were told to follow me. The criminal they were to arrest was the man that I would kiss.

I felt horribly conspicuous as I walked in front of my little army of ruffians, many of whose muttered curses and complaints I could hear above the tramp of their feet. Mercifully, the streets were dark and almost deserted, and it was not far from the Temple to the city gates. Soon we were outside and marching down the hill to the Garden of Gethsemane. My heart pounding, I prayed that everything would go to plan.

The light from the torches illuminated the trees as we walked through the garden, and the gnarled branches cast sinister shadows on the ground. Eventually we came to a clearing, and there, on a small hillock, stood the Master. You and Darius stood on either side of him, watching our approach. James and John were there too, their faces wild with terror, as they frantically appealed for the Master to flee. As we got closer they lost all courage and ran for their lives away into the darkness.

I halted the troop of police with a raised hand, and they waited silently for my identification. The Master's face was calm, and he looked at me expectantly. You had a sword in your hand, Peter, and I know you would have used it to protect the Master's life. Darius's eyes were expressionless, and my heart went out to him. Stepping forward, I greeted him as Master, embraced him tenderly and kissed him.

Instantly, we were surrounded by the Temple police who dragged Darius roughly from my arms and shackled his wrists with chains. I ordered them to leave the other two men. They had the one they had come for and they did as I commanded. In no time at all, Darius was bound and being marched sway. Before following, I glanced quickly at the Master. There was a look of shocked astonishment on his face as he gazed after the disappearing Darius. Guiltily, I turned and ran to catch up with police and prisoner.

We were soon in the courtyard before the grand mansion of Caiaphas, where we were ordered to wait for the arrival of the Sanhedrin members who had been summoned for the trial.

The police gathered around a charcoal fire to warm themselves and servants brought out hot spiced wine for them. They drank and made lewd remarks to the serving wenches. I kept myself apart, for though I was cold I found their company too loathsome to share the heat with them.

One guard began to curse Darius for causing them to lose a night's sleep, and the others agreed with him in surly voices. Another went up to Darius, who was standing quietly by, head bowed and wrists still bound, and ordered him to apologize to them. He made no reply, and the man spat contemptuously in his face. The others called him vile names and jeered at his silent meekness. One pulled a length of dirty cloth out from his tunic and, blindfolding Darius with it, winked at the others, saying the man was a prophet, and knew things that others did not. He spun him around and slapped his face, telling him to prophesy who had struck him. Enjoying the joke, and laughing uproariously, the others formed a circle around Darius, pushing him and spinning him and hitting him. I stepped forward and protested at their behaviour, telling them to stop, but they snarled that I might be next if I didn't shut up, being equally to blame for their missed slumber.

Darius made no sound as he was whirled around like a limp doll between them, and his passivity seemed to enrage them all the more, for they became like savages, kicking, spitting and punching him with heavy blows, and swearing in the foulest of terms. Blood poured from Darius's nose and mouth, but he uttered not one word.

Eventually the men grew bored with their game and returned to the fire, the chief bully retrieving his blindfold and roughly wiping the blood from Darius's face with it. And still he retained his patient silence. The bravery of the man astounded me, right to the end.

It was then that I saw you, Peter, peering into the courtyard from the street outside. I went to the gatekeeper and told him to admit you, and he did so, asking if you were one of the prisoner's followers, which you denied. Puzzlement was written on your face, but I whispered that I would explain all to you later, and that we should not be seen together.

You muttered that the Master had returned to the room at Joseph's house and ordered me to report to him there. We parted furtively, you going to join the group around the fire, where I heard you again hotly deny that you had anything to do with their captive.

Then the doors of the house were opened and we were called to enter. Darius, flanked by two guards, was escorted in and led to the centre of a huge hall, around which a ring of High Priests were seated, yawning and peevish for having been called from their beds.

The priest with whom I had made the bargain met me at the door, and he handed me a purse of coins, telling me that I could count them if I wished, but all thirty pieces of silver were there. Our business was concluded. I decided to stay and watch the proceedings, making myself as inconspicuous as possible by standing in the shadow of a pillar behind the assembled High Priests.

Darius, as I had advised, remained silent to all questions and accusations that were hurled at him. A handful of false witnesses were brought forward and made various statements about his deeds and teaching, claiming that he had set himself up as the Messiah and demanded the worship of the people, but none of them had ever seen the Master in the flesh and could only speak from hearsay, and there were many contradictions in their reports. One claimed that he had said the Temple should be destroyed, which caused a ripple of angry muttering among the priests, but nothing definite could be proved against him, and I was beginning to hope that they might have to release him through lack of evidence, when the Chief High Priest, Caiaphas, stood up.

A portly figure with a massive beard, he strutted around Darius, glaring, his eyebrows knitted in a fierce frown. He asked why he did not speak. Had he nothing to say to all these accusations? Darius remained silent, his eyes on the floor. Then Caiaphas commanded him to answer one question. Was he Christ, the Son of God?

Slowly, Darius raised his head and stared in Caiaphas's face. Then he spoke. His voice was quiet, but clear. Yes, he said. He was.

Over the gasps of horror and angry oaths Caiaphas's voice boomed in triumph. Blasphemy! What need was there for further witnesses? They had all heard the blasphemy from his own lips. What was their verdict?

In a unanimous chorus the priests said that he should die. Many rose from their seats and surrounded Darius, spitting at him and slapping him. It was announced that he was to be taken before Pontius Pilate, the Roman procurator, to be officially sentenced to death. The doors of the hall were thrown open, and out they all swept in malicious glee, Darius being pushed and pinched and jostled in their midst.

In the lowest of spirits I made my way to the Upper City as dawn was breaking. If he had only kept silent he might have been saved! Why had he said the one thing that was bound to inflame them the most? It was almost as though he wanted to die.

As I entered the courtyard of Joseph's house I suddenly realized that he had not been present at the trial. In fact many Sanhedrin members had been absent, at such short notice it would have been difficult to summon them all together. I wondered what Joseph's reaction would have been if had he been there and seen Darius tried in place of the Master.

I climbed the steps to the room and knocked with great trepidation at the door, which was bolted from the inside. Receiving no reply, I put my mouth to a crack and whispered my name. The bolt grated out and the door swung open. It was shut and bolted again by the Master once I had entered, and he stared at me coldly and accusingly in the gloom. He asked me to explain myself. I stammered that it had been Darius' idea, not mine. I had confided in him and we had both agreed that the Master would have been in mortal danger. It was Darius who had suggested taking his place. I told him how he had been treated by the police, saying that I would rather have died than hand over the Master to such barbarians.

He covered his face with his hands and whispered Darius's name in a voice full of despair. Then turning to me fiercely, he said that I had broken my promise. Again I had acted behind his back. After giving my word to do as I was commanded, I had deliberately defied him. He loved Darius more than a brother, and it was I who was responsible for the suffering he had endured. He rued the day he had taken me as a disciple and he would never trust me again.

I begged him to believe we had merely conspired together to spare him pain and humiliation. I sobbed out the story of the trial and the charge of blasphemy and the taking of Darius to Pilate. Frantically, I held out the purse of money that I had received from the priests, but he backed away in horror, as though I were offering him a handful of scorpions.

Flinging open the door, he told me to take the money back

and tell them I had handed over the wrong man. Conscience had gotten the better of me, I had cheated them, I repented, and they must release him. Darius must be saved at all costs!

Babbling that I would do my best, and reminding him of the chance of pardon at the Passover amnesty, I seized his hand and covered it with kisses, but he pulled it away and wiped it on his tunic as though it were polluted. He told me to go without delay. If Darius were to die, he would hold me alone responsible.

I flew through the streets like a maniac, the purse of coins clutched tightly in my hand. Reaching the Temple, I observed no formalities, but charged down the private corridors that I had already twice visited, pushing aside those who tried to obstruct me. The startled and indignant faces of the High Priests looked up as I burst into their room, and I panted out my message. The man they had was innocent. It was not the Master who they had condemned. They had been misled. I had cheated them and was sorry. They must release him and I would return the money. I held out the purse with trembling hands.

They looked at me scornfully, one suppressing a bored yawn. He said that it didn't matter. The one I had delivered to them suited their purposes. He had openly claimed to be the Messiah and was therefore guilty of the heinous crime of blasphemy. The process of the law had been generated and could not be halted. I had earned my reward and could keep it. My guilty conscience was no concern of theirs.

Disdainfully, they returned to the counting of their gold. Enraged at my impotence, I tore open the purse and flung the silver coins down. The cling and clatter as they bounced and rolled across the marble floor, disturbed one priest enough to click his fingers and bring two guards to my side, who, gripped my arms and forcibly escorted me from the chamber, while I ranted over my shoulder that they must release their innocent captive. They threw me out into the sunlight on the Temple steps.

Stumbling to my feet, I made my way down to the Praetorium, where the Passover amnesty was to be announced.

The large courtyard in front of the building was packed with people waiting to petition Pilate. Roman guards stood on the steps, spears in hand, their faces stony and impassive. I pushed my way through the impatient crowd, and when I was near the front everyone fell silent as Pilate emerged from the palace.

Behind him came Darius, flanked by two soldiers. He was almost unrecognizable.

Branches of thorns had been fashioned into a crown and placed on his head, the spikes digging into his brow, from which rivulets of blood ran. His eyelids were puffed; his lips swollen and split and his nose askew, as though it had been broken. A purple cloak which had been thrown around his shoulders did not disguise the fact that he had been scourged, for it stuck to the raw bloody lash strokes on his back. His body swayed as though he might fall at any moment. He was a sickening sight and I pitied him deeply, but I thanked God that it was he and not the Master who stood there.

Pilate raised his hand to silence the curious and excited muttering that had been aroused by Darius. He announced that the Sanhedrin had demanded the punishment of this prisoner for blasphemy and as they could see, that it had obviously been carried out. But after questioning the man he could find no criminal charges to bring against him, and since he had the power to release one prisoner to them on that day, would they not wish it to be this one—the self-styled "King of the Jews"?

At this a great murmuring spread through the crowd and there was a chorus of protest from the front ranks. Standing on tiptoe I could see that it came from a cadre of High Priests who had been at Darius's trial. They demanded that he be crucified. When Pilate asked them why, they shouted that he had made himself out to be the Son of God, and according to Jewish law he should die. They warned Pilate that he should think of his own position. Anyone who claimed such a title was placing himself above Caesar. If he released him, Caesar would not be pleased.

Pilate turned and spoke quietly to Darius. I strained to hear his words, but it was impossible over the growing, impatient hubbub of the crowd. Darius did not answer anyway. He seemed oblivious to his surroundings; his gaze fixed on nothing. The group of priests continued in chorus to demand his crucifixion.

Pilate turned again to the crowd and raised his hand for silence, asking them to select the prisoner they wished to be released.

The courtyard immediately echoed with raised voices calling the names of those they wanted to be set free, and I added mine, shouting the name of the Master as loudly as I could, but my voice was drowned by the majority, who chanted in unison for the release of Barabbas. I heard no other calls of the Master's name, and realizing that I was wasting my breath, I nudged the man chanting next to me and asked him who Barabbas was. He broke off to tell me that he was a Zealot who had recently been arrested during an anti-Roman demonstration in the city, a great freedom fighter—far more worthy of reprieve than the pacifist nobody that Pilate was trying to palm them off with. Then he resumed the chant and the whole courtyard resounded with the name of Barabbas. Barabbas! Barabbas! Barabbas! I could hear no other. My heart sank. Darius hadn't a chance.

Pilate raised his hand but the volume of the chanting increased and showed no sign of abating. Eventually, Pilate spoke briefly to a guard who marched into the palace and returned shortly with a bearded grinning ruffian who was greeted with wild cheers. After being unshackled by Pilate he raised his fists in triumph and bounded down the steps to be mobbed and feted by the jubilant crowd, who carried him shoulder-high out of the courtyard like a king. After washing his hands in a bowl held by a slave, Pilate went back into the Praetorium followed by Darius and his guards.

I approached a Roman soldier and asked him what would be done with Darius. He replied that he would be executed outside the city walls at Golgotha, along with another couple of criminals.

Then he told me to be on my way. The prisoner of popular choice had been released and the entertainment was over.

Sick at heart, I wandered aimlessly through the streets until I came to the square before the Temple, where I sat on a step, head in hands, almost deaf to the cries of the traders and moneychangers, and the usual frenetic bustle of Sabbath-eve going on around me. Darius was to die, the Master despised me, everything was ruined—but who cared? The selfish world went on.

Eventually I pulled myself together, and realizing that I had no alternative but to face the Master with the news, I rose and made my way to the Upper City with footsteps as heavy as my heart.

It was then that I met you, Peter, coming down the street. We stopped and stared at one another for some time before speaking. I read puzzlement and distrust in your eyes. I don't know what you read in mine. I told you that Darius was to be crucified, and I was going to inform the Master. You told me that he already knew.

Instructed by him to be there, you had been in the crowded courtyard before the Praetorium, witnessed the release of Barabbas, and hurried back to inform the Master of Darius's fate. The news had distressed him greatly and he had wept. On gaining composure, he had given several orders, the first of which you had already carried out.

You had gone to Joseph of Arimathea, told him that the Master had been condemned to be crucified for blasphemy, and begged him to ask Pilate for the body after death. Joseph, already mounted in preparation at the time for an appointment in Capernaum, had been shocked by the news, and promised that he would send servants acting in his name to Pilate, and have the corpse laid in his own private tomb until he returned. Expressing deep regret over the loss of the Master, he had set off on his journey without delay, in order to arrive before the Sabbath dawn.

You had also been instructed to forbid any brother to attend the crucifixion of "the Master", and return to Galilee to await further orders. You had sworn to reveal to no one the truth of what happened in the garden. You warned me that the Master would be far from pleased to see me at that time. Utterly dejected, I turned and retraced my steps to the Lower City in your company.

You tried to question me on the way. Could I explain why Darius had been arrested, and why he had pretended to be the Master? You were to inform the others that it was the Master who had been captured and crucified—news that would horrify and dismay them—whereas the truth that he was safe and free would cause them to rejoice. You were deeply confused.

I told you to follow the Master's instructions and be patient. All would be revealed in time. That time is now, Peter. I have related the facts to you to the best of my ability, but there is more to follow. My story is almost ended, and soon everything will be clear to you.

We parted in the Temple Square; you gave me one last puzzled frown, before turning with a deep sigh and disappearing into the crowd, on your way back to Galilee. I fought an impulse to run after you and explain everything there and then. I knew that you would understand and forgive me. But my lips were sealed.

> *There were also women looking on afar off..*
> Mark 15:40

> *women were there beholding afar off...*
> Matthew 27:55

> *women that followed him from Galilee, stood afar off, beholding these things.*
> Luke 23:49

I decided to go out to Golgotha and witness the crucifixion, just in case Darius broke down and revealed our secret, although I was sure he would carry it with him to the grave. He had proved himself the most stalwart of disciples. I made my way to the East Gate and out into the hilly countryside.

Golgotha is not far from the city, and climbing an escarpment, I came in sight of three crosses in the distance. The victims hanging on them were naked, and although it was too far away to make out their faces, I could plainly hear their agonized groans. The figure on the middle cross was silent, though he slowly writhed in pain. I knew that it was Darius.

A group of Roman centurions squatted on the ground before him playing dice, laughing and swearing. How I detested them! I would have given my soul to be able to rush forward and slaughter them, pull out the nails which pinioned Darius's hands, lift him gently down from the cross, and tell him his ordeal was over. But there was nothing in the world that I could do but stand there staring in speechless rage.

Suddenly, I heard the sound of sobbing, and looking down from the cliff on which I stood, I saw two women below me. I recognized them at once as Mary and the Master's mother. The latter was weeping bitterly, and Mary held her in her arms, comforting her.

Not wishing to be seen, I lay down on the cliff edge and peered cautiously over. I guessed that the fleeing brothers must have called at Bethany on their way back to Galilee with them news of the Master's arrest, and the women had come to witness his end. Darius was too far away to be identified, and they were convinced that his crucified body was that of the Master.

The mother began to beat her breast and scream accusations at herself, crying that it was her fault he had come to such an end. Mary tried to quieten her, telling her that she was talking nonsense, but the mother insisted. He had been brought up believing that he was different from others, special to God, and she had been responsible.

Mary said that she had heard the marvelous rumors of his conception, but had not dared to question her about them. The mother stopped crying and wiped her eyes. Then, in a tired voice, she told Mary her tale. I relate it here for you without personal comment.

It had happened in her village, Nazareth, when she was hardly more than a girl, thirteen or fourteen years of age. Her father drank, was bad tempered and occasionally beat her, so she was looking forward to her coming marriage to Joseph the carpenter, a kind and pious man, although many years her senior, as a means of escape.

It was her duty to go and fetch water early every morning before the rest of the family was awake. One morning she had gone as usual, and found a Roman soldier seated by the well. At first she had been afraid, alone with a foreigner, but he had smiled at her, asked for a drink, and was charming and handsome. She had tarried; amused by his blundering pronunciation of her language and the strange sounds he made in his own, and fascinated by the blueness of his eyes.

Suddenly he had caught her in a firm embrace from which she

could not escape, and murmuring fond endearments, had carried her to a copse nearby and done things which, after the initial fear and pain, had filled her with a mysterious pleasure.

When it was over, and he lay spent by her side, realizing how late it had become, and fearing the wrath of her father, she had hastily rearranged her clothing, gathered her pitcher from beside the well, and returned speedily home before the family had risen.

She never saw the soldier again, but fondly remembered his caresses and kisses, until she soon realized that something was wrong with her body. To her horror, she discovered that she was with child.

Not daring to tell her father, for fear of being beaten to death, she had gone to her fiancé Joseph with the only explanation she could think of to save herself. She said that an angel had appeared to her and announced that she was to bear the Son of God.

Her virtue unquestionable, Joseph had believed the story and hastened the wedding forward, saving her life and reputation. The Master had been born, and when he was old enough to understand, Joseph had taken him aside and told him of the angel and the message.

And so he had grown up in the belief that he was the Chosen One, destined to establish his Father's Kingdom on Earth. Mary had kept silent on the matter, afraid that the truth would turn him against her. But now she wished to God she had confided in him. Even if he had hated her, he would have been spared this vile and pointless death.

Mary kissed her and told her that she was wrong to blame herself. His parentage made no difference. The Master was truly a great man and teacher. He had chosen his path and nothing could have deflected him from it. He had been destined to die this way.

In the distance, Darius broke his silence with a long wail of agony.

"Why have you deserted me?"

Then he was quiet.

Thick black clouds appeared on the horizon, blotting out the sun and bringing a swirling wind. A storm was on its way.

Another woman appeared and joined the others. It was Martha. She had been searching the streets of Jerusalem for any remaining disciples, but had found none. All had fled like cowards. Lazarus and his wife were not at home either, having left town to visit her relatives in Decapolis for Passover. There was no one to help them.

A final cry from Darius was borne on the wind. It sounded ecstatic, almost triumphant

"It is accomplished!" he screamed, and then slumped forward. I knew that he was dead, and I thanked God that his suffering was over.

The Roman guards, irritated by the gusts of sand that stung their bare legs, began preparing to return to the city. Sabbath was about to begin, and, it being forbidden for Jews to be left on crosses over the Holy Day, they took hammers and smashed the legs of the two men on either side of Darius, laughing at their agonized screams, before pulling them down and leaving them to crawl away and die. They did not break Darius's legs. He being already dead, it wasn't worth the effort. But one soldier, just to make certain, took his spear and jabbed it into his ribcage, causing the women to shriek with horror.

As they were taking down his body, two men approached and began talking to the soldiers. One gave them a scroll and the soldiers handed over the corpse to them, which they wrapped in a sheet, picked up and began to carry away. I guessed that they were Joseph's servants and had shown the guards a letter of permission from Pilate for them to collect the body. They were taking it to store in Joseph's private tomb. The women were puzzled, and decided to follow and find out where the body was to be laid.

I followed too, keeping enough distance between us to avoid detection, but the women did not look back, intent as they were on keeping the corpse in sight.

The men entered a small garden just outside the city walls. Concealing myself behind a tree, I watched them enter a tomb in the rock cliff, dump the body without ceremony and emerge wiping their hands on their tunics. After rolling a large stone across the entrance, they went away together, ignoring the women who stood silent at a distance, staring at the tomb.

When the men had gone the women agreed together that they would return the day after the Sabbath to wash and anoint the body of the Master properly for burial. As they left the garden a jagged sword of lightning illuminated the sky, followed by a tremendous crack of thunder and the first tepid drops of a heavy rainfall.

I remained under the shelter of the trees, staring at the coverstone, blessing Darius for his sacrifice and saying a prayer for his soul. Meanwhile the storm increased its fury, and with each lightning flash and roar of thunder it was as if God was expressing his anger and outrage at what had been done.

And then suddenly, just as a particularly brilliant flash whitened the sky, a new idea came to me, and by the time the crash of thunder had rumbled away, it had all been laid out in my mind. Tears of joy welled from my eyes, mingling with the rain on my cheeks as I ran out under it, crying and laughing at the same time.

God had given me a plan that would save our seemingly hopelessly lost cause and bring new converts in flocks, droves, and millions! I threw wild kisses to the sky as I hurried from the garden and into the city, drenched to the skin and dancing ecstatically in the overflowing gutters.

> *But Thomas, one of the twelve, called Didymus,*
> *was not with them when Jesus came.*
> *The other disciples therefore said unto him, We have*
> *seen the Lord. But he said unto them, Except I shall*
> *see in his hands the print of the nails, and put my*
> *finger into the print of the nails, and thrust my*
> *hand into his side, I will not believe.*
> John 20:24-5

I was soon in Joseph's courtyard in the Upper City, but my high excitement dwindled away to nervousness as I mounted the steps to the room above the stable. Again I found the door locked, and had to knock hard and call the Master's name before I heard it unbolted, and then push it open for myself.

The room was gloomy, lit only by a single lamp. The Master stood before me, his face in shadow. He stared at me without a trace of emotion, as though I was nothing, and it was dreadful to me. I begged him to speak—abuse me, condemn me—anything but that wordless stare.

He spoke in a voice as cold as ice. I had murdered his dearest friend, he said, destroyed the mission and perverted the prophecies. He preached forgiveness, but never could he find it in his heart to forgive me for what I had done.

If it had not been for me, I blurted out, he would have been the one crucified. Darius had gone willingly to his death to spare him. He would have been proud to see how bravely he had died! "Greater love has no man than to lay down his life for his friend." He had said that and Darius had done it, and there would be jubilation in Heaven at his arrival instead of the Master, who still had so much left to perform in this world!

He turned away from me with a groan, burying his face in his hands, and in a tone of the deepest despair said that it should have been him and not Darius. All was finished!

I replied firmly that it was not. In a way it was only the beginning. And quickly I began to relate the plan that had come to me outside the tomb.

Darius was dead and the Master was alive, yet everyone believed that it was he who had been arrested, tried and executed on the cross. This was the God-given chance to establish himself once and for all as the true Messiah. Removing his hands from his face, he sat down on a bench, telling me to leave, as my presence and the sound of my voice sickened him. Undaunted, I continued.

He was alive, and none but Peter and I knew it. He had raised Lazarus from the dead, with many witnesses to testify. If he wished, he could now perform the ultimate miracle of his career. He could stage his own resurrection!

He looked at me, comprehension slowly dawning. I said that if he should reveal himself after the Sabbath, whole and well, unvanquished even by Death, who could refuse to believe that he was truly the anointed One, the Son of God? Even the High Priests and the Romans would be awestruck and afraid. All was not finished. He should seize the opportunity that Darius had given him by his willing self-sacrifice.

After a long silence, the Master reminded me of the body. It lay in the tomb and could easily be produced as evidence by his enemies. Laughing, I said that it was no problem. Due to the storm and the Sabbath, nobody was abroad that night. I would return to the garden, remove the corpse and carry it to the nearby refuse tip where it would soon be disposed of by the wild dogs which scavenged there.

In a horrified voice he asked how I could do such a thing. Slightly impatient, I pointed out that Darius was dead. He had served his purpose, and his soul was certainly with God. He had no further use for his body and it had to disappear if the plan were to succeed. I told him of the women's intention to anoint the body the day after Sabbath. The Master should appear to them outside the empty tomb, and they would be the first witnesses of his return to life. The word would spread that he had risen, was invincible, omnipotent, and it would surely be the dawning of the Kingdom.

Kneeling before him and kissing his hands, I begged forgiveness for the pain I had unwillingly caused him. I was his devoted slave. My life was nothing without him.

Extricating his hands from my grasp, he told me to do what I had to do. Past experience had shown him that once I was set upon a scheme not even he could prevent me from carrying it out. I rose to my feet eagerly and made for the door, promising that I would return to inform him when the deed had been accomplished, but he stopped me, saying that there was a small task for me before I left, and after rummaging among a pile of tools in the corner he turned to me, holding out a heavy mallet and a long, sharp nail.

I understood his intention and my blood froze. I exclaimed that it would not be necessary. He looked at me scornfully, and in a voice of granite replied that it was necessary if we were to be convincing. He would be brave.

Seating himself on the bench, he placed his right hand palm-upward on the rough wood, offering me the hammer and nail with his left. I backed away in revulsion. I could not do it, I cried. The thought of causing the Master physical pain and scarring his blessed body with my own hands was abhorrent to me.

A look of dark fury swept his face, and he spat out his words. After the long, appalling torture that Darius had endured for his sake, did I think that he was incapable of bearing a couple of paltry wounds? Flinging the implements to the floor, he commanded me to leave. My company revolted him. I had thwarted him all along, acting behind his back and disobeying his orders. Even this last simple request I refused to perform. I was a traitor, a coward, and he detested me.

I could not stand his accusations. They were so unjust and untrue. I reached down for the discarded tools and, taking them up, approached him, trembling. The anger left his face, and he looked at me almost lovingly. He told me to strike hard and quickly, and I held the nail over his unflinching palm with the mallet above it, unable to move, as though paralyzed. He leaned forward and kissed me gently on the cheek, telling me not to be afraid. Let me show that I loved him enough to follow an order that I loathed to perform.

Summoning up all my strength, I smashed the hammer down on the nail and felt it pass through his hand into the wood beneath. The Master screamed and I became hysterical, sobbing and jabbering, begging him to forgive me, but fiercely he demanded that I pull the nail out swiftly and do the other hand. I obeyed him, wild with grief at the spilling of his precious blood.

The task accomplished, I lay at the Master's feet, weeping and hating myself for what I had done. Gradually, as my sobs subsided, I became aware of the profound silence in the room, and looking up I saw the Master gazing in fascination at the crimson blood that oozed and dripped from his open wounds. As though in a trance, and without raising his eyes, he told me to go and never to let him see my face again. He would never forgive me for as long as he lived for handing over Darius instead of him.

Realizing the futility of argument, I crawled to the door, broken-hearted. Before letting myself out, I turned to take my last glimpse of the Master. He sat there staring at his bleeding palms and whispering the name of Darius over and over again.

> *Now when Jesus was risen early the first day of the week, he appeared first to Mary Magdalene, out of whom he had cast seven devils.*
> *And she went and told them that had been with him, as they mourned and wept.*
> *And they, when they had heard that he was alive, and had been seen of her, believed not.*
> Mark 16:9-11

The storm had not abated, but I was hardly aware of it as I walked through the deserted, rain-lashed streets. My mind had become numb, fixed on the mutilation I had performed on the Master, and my banishment from his company forever.

I made my way out of the city to the garden tomb. There, after brief panic when the stone refused to budge against the pressure of my shoulder, I found a fallen branch, using it as a lever, and slowly managed to move it aside. Entering the tomb, I was struck by the smell and silence of death. I gathered the corpse in my arms, dragged it out into the rain and heaved it onto my shoulder. It was surprisingly light but cumbersome, and I staggered out to the city rubbish dumps, the wind whipping and wailing around me.

I laid it in a desolate place where I could hear the nearby howling of wild dogs on the prowl. Stripping off the winding-sheet, I looked down at Darius's pale, blood-caked body lying there in the mud and garbage. Tears came to my eyes, and I asked the forgiveness of his departed soul. I was sure that he would have approved of my plan. Perhaps even, in that flash of lightning, the inspiration had come from him.

Another bolt streaked across the sky and I saw three mangy curs approaching with cunning stealth down the hillside, their eyes gleaming hungrily. I turned and walked quickly away, leaving them to their supper.

I returned to the tomb and replaced the winding-cloth on the slab. I sat there for a while, sheltering from the storm and pondering the fate of Darius, the rich young man who had given up all his wealth to follow the Master and find eternal life, only to suffer the ignominious death of a criminal and be devoured by dogs on a rubbish tip.

As for me, I knew that my part in the story was over. Against my will it had been my lot to be cast as the villain, and I would be remembered and vilified as such long after my death, as the Master's name and message spread throughout the land. His life and deeds would be recorded and elaborated upon, and I knew that for the legend of his death and resurrection to grow, I must always be known as the traitor who had sold him for a handful of coins. It had to be so.

And Darius . . . he would not—must not—be remembered for the role he had played in saving the Master's life. No one knew of it but the Master and myself – and you Peter. A wave of panic swept over me, but soon subsided. I was more than positive that you would keep the secret.

I thought of my future. It was necessary for me to disappear completely from the scene for events to proceed smoothly. I contemplated suicide, but the idea terrified me. And I needed to be certain that the Master would begin the new chapter by revealing his resurrected self with the wounds I had so unwillingly inflicted upon him. If he did not do that everything would have been in vain, especially the death of Darius.

After a while the storm passed over and the sky became clear. The stars seemed washed, so clearly did they shine, and the wind dropped to a faint breeze. I left the tomb and moved to a part of the garden where I could keep it in view without being seen myself. Lying down on the sodden grass beneath a tree, I fell into an exhausted, dreamless sleep.

I slept throughout the whole of the Sabbath day. There was

nothing else to do. Waking occasionally, I remembered where I was and what I had done, and swiftly sought again the blissful oblivion of sleep. The sun dried out my clothes. When night fell I rose and ate some figs and berries from the trees. Then I sat and waited for the dawn. I was utterly and completely alone, but that night I could summon up no emotion, not even self-pity.

The women arrived just as the sun was rising, carrying towels and vessels of water and myrrh. Concealed by some bushes, I watched and listened. The mother, weary from the journey, put down her pitcher and sank to the ground, asking them to rest a while before opening the tomb. It would require all their strength, and that, along with the grief that they were to spend thereafter, would leave them totally exhausted. Martha sat and put a comforting arm around her. Mary, bidding them rest, said that she would go and see how difficult it was to move the stone. She returned a few moments later, crying that the tomb was open and empty. Someone had stolen the Master's body!

Martha and the mother rose and, telling Mary to stay and guard the myrrh, they hurried off to see if what she said was true. Mary covered her face with her hands and began to weep in despair.

Suddenly my heart leapt with joy. The Master had emerged from behind a tree and was approaching her. His face was partly covered by a scarf, and his hands were bandaged. He came to her side and asked her why she was crying. She wheeled around and, not recognizing him, asked that if he had removed the Master's body she beseeched him to show her where it was so that it could be properly anointed before burial.

He spoke her name, and with a shock she realized who he was. Falling to the ground, she stretched out her arms, but he backed away, telling her not to touch him. As she gazed up in astonished rapture, he told her to tell the others that she had seen him. They should return to Galilee, where he would shortly come to them and give further instructions.

He turned to go, but Mary begged him to stay and show himself to his mother. Scrambling to her feet, she ran towards the tomb calling to the others. As soon as she had gone the Master walked quickly away out of the garden.

Mary returned pulling the other two by their hands, but stopped in dismay when she saw that he was gone. She looked around in bewilderment. The Master had been there, she stammered. He had talked to her. She had touched him.

The mother said that she must have imagined it. The shock of finding the tomb empty had been too much for her. Martha tried to put an arm around her, but Mary shook her off, saying that she had not imagined it. The Master was alive! He had risen! Truly risen from the grave! She must go to Galilee and tell the disciples! Laughing and clapping her hands, she danced joyfully out of the garden. Martha and the mother looked at each other and sadly shook their heads before following her; the mother reverently clutching the bloodstained sheet which had wrapped the body of Darius.

I remained in the garden for the rest of the day, not knowing what to do. I was overjoyed that the Master had shown himself to Mary, but disappointed that Martha and his mother had not also seen him. They believed Mary to have suddenly lost her wits, and so would the disciples if they did not see him in person. I prayed that he would appear to them.

Night came, and I felt totally lost. Where could I go? What could I do? Life without the Master was meaningless to me. Although banished forever from his presence, I had to be somewhere I could at least hear news of his progress.

And so it was that I decided to return to Bethany and throw myself on the mercy of Martha and Mary. They were my oldest friends, and although they might hate me now for what they believed I had done, I knew they would not turn me away. Mary might even welcome me, knowing as she did that the Master was alive.

The village was dark and silent when I arrived. I rapped quietly on the shutter of Martha's bedroom window and she opened it after a while and peered out. She gasped when she saw me, and a look of undisguised disgust came over her face. I begged her to let me in, and she came and opened the courtyard door. I entered quickly and she closed it behind me. Staring at me coldly, she demanded an explanation. I asked how much she already knew.

She told me that a couple of days before, James and John and several other brothers had arrived in the early hours of the morning in a state of fearful excitement with the tale that I had led a troop of police to the garden where the Master was sleeping and supervised his arrest. They had fled after delivering the news, fearing that they were being pursued, saying that the Master was doomed and the mission over. She, Mary and the mother had set off for the city at once to find out what had happened, but by the time they had got there it was all over.

Inquiring at the Temple, they had learned the charge of blasphemy, the place of execution, and that it was I who had betrayed him. They had hurried to Golgotha, knowing that there was nothing they could do to save him, and watched helplessly from a distance while the Master had died a horrible and agonizing death. They had followed two strangers who had taken the body, and seen where it was laid. Returning again the day after the Sabbath, with the intention of anointing the body, they found that it had been removed from the tomb. The grief had been too much for Mary and she had lost her mind. They had returned to Bethany trying to calm her, but she insisted that the Master was alive and had appeared to her and that she must go to Galilee to tell the men that he was coming. She could not be controlled, and to humor her, she had been allowed to set off there that evening, in the company of the mother.

Again she asked me to account for my behavior. How could I, who had professed to love him so much, have handed the Master over to the authorities for a wretched thirty pieces of silver? I told her that I could not explain. I knelt before her, weeping and begging her forgiveness, and pleading with her to hide me. Disgusted though she was by my treachery, she said that she would give me sanctuary for the sake of the Master, to put into deed his teaching on forgiveness, even to a miserable traitor like myself. She took me to Lazarus's empty tomb at the end of the garden, and we made arrangements for my daily existence.

That is my story, Peter. It is finished, and I wonder what you will make of it?

Dawn has broken. The patch of sky visible through the gap is getting lighter. Tonight, when Martha comes with my supper, I will ask her to send for you to come to me. There will be no need for conversation. I will simply hand you this manuscript, and when you have read it you will tell me whether what I did was right or wrong. I will trust your judgement. You may even he able to petition the Master for me when he returns and bring about a reconciliation between us. No, such a hope is beyond expectation. I must force myself now to lay down my writing and say I am in your hands.

Your loving brother,

Judas Iscariot.

> *Fear them not therefore: for there is nothing covered, that shall not be revealed; and hid, that shall not he known.*
> Matthew 10:26

I am writing again. It helps to pass the time and focus my mind, which otherwise keeps returning to images of the Master's bleeding hands, his harsh accusations and stern, unforgiving face.

Martha was surprised last night when I told her to send for Peter in Jerusalem, and asked why I wanted to see him. I told her that I could not reveal the reason, hut I begged her to do it. I asked her to say that it is she who urgently wishes to speak to him and not to mention my name. When he arrives she should inform him where I am and tell him to come to me. She stared at me suspiciously. Then, with a shrug, she said that she would send a servant to the city the following day.

As she was leaving she noticed my epistle on the slab. She stopped and asked what I had been writing. I said that it was just some psalms I had memorized in my youth, which I had written down to kill the time. She reached for the pages, asking if she could read them, but I snatched them away quickly and clutched them to my breast, stammering out excuses. She would not be able to read my handwriting; my spelling was bad; some of the lines I had forgotten and omitted, making the verses unsatisfactory and difficult to understand. She could not read them. They were private.

She looked at me searchingly with a strange expression that made me look away. I was sweating. I could not let her read the letter. No one must know the truth but Peter and me.

"So be it," she said in a cold voice. If what I had written was so unsuitable for her eyes she would not insist. She left, saying that she would instruct Peter to come and visit her the next evening, leaving me cursing myself for having aroused her curiosity in my document. She will surely inform Peter of it before he comes to see me.

That was last night. Now as I write, I expect his arrival at any moment. What will be his reaction to my testament? It was not my initial intention to write to him at all. I desired the writing material to relieve my monotony and despair, but on learning of his return to Jerusalem I developed an overwhelming urge to let him know everything as I remember it, and it is better this way, without having to look into his eyes and answer his puzzled questions, which I would have to do if I related my story verbally. That would be too painful and laborious.

I believe he is coming! Through the gap I can see a lantern swinging through the darkness towards me from the far end of the garden! My throat is dry and my heart is beating fast with excitement. I must stop now and greet him. When he has finished reading I am certain that he will understand and forgive me.

I can't understand. I don't believe it. It is only an hour or so since I saw the approaching light of the lantern. Certain that it was Peter, I stopped writing and waited for him to enter the tomb. Nobody entered. Instead, the stone before the entrance began to move, and before I knew what was happening it had ground to a halt and sealed me inside. I ran and tried to push it back, but there are no finger-holds and it is impossible to budge. I have tried and tried. My fingernails are broken and bleeding and I am exhausted.

It is a joke. It must be a joke. I will wait and laugh with Peter when he moves the stone aside again soon.

The flame in the lamp is beginning to die and it is becoming difficult to breathe.

If it is a joke then it has gone too far.

I have tried shouting and screaming but my voice has gone.

Perhaps it wasn't Peter.

Martha knows I am here. Tomorrow she will come as usual with my supper.

She must have told him about the letter.

Yes. That must be it. I knew Peter could be trusted. So loyal. So protective! The secret is safe and locked away. Locked away in the tomb.

It is not a joke. The light is nearly gone, a flicker, the bread and wine are gone long ago.

I cannot endure.

Why did he not give me the chance?

The light has gone. I write in blackness. Utter. It is finished. Accomplished. Air gone. Forgive me.

Master . . .

Printed in the United States
2150